D0426430

# A
# WARNING
# ABOUT
# SWANS

Published by Peachtree Teen
An imprint of PEACHTREE PUBLISHING COMPANY INC.
1700 Chattahoochee Avenue
Atlanta, Georgia 30318-2112
*PeachtreeBooks.com*

Edited by Ashley Hearn
Design and composition by Lily Steele

**Content Warnings: Animal death, physical and psychological abuse,
emotional manipulation**

Printed and bound in May 2023 at Lake Book Manufacturing, Melrose Park, IL, USA.
10 9 8 7 6 5 4 3 2 1
First Edition
ISBN: 978-1-68263-483-7

Library of Congress Cataloging-in-Publication Data

Names: Romero, R. M. (Rachael Maria), 1987- author.
Title: A warning about swans / R.M. Romero.
Description: Atlanta : Peachtree Teen, 2023. | Audience: Ages 14 and up. |
    Audience: Grades 10-12. | Summary: Swan maiden Hilde sacrifices her
    magical wings to seek freedom in the human world, but when her pact with
    an upstart baron takes her the court of Ludwig II, she struggles to fit
    in, and only Jewish artist Franz, who has the power to paint souls, can
    help her escape her newfound prison.
Identifiers: LCCN 2022056188 | ISBN 9781682634837 (hardcover) | ISBN
    9781682635155 (ebook)
Subjects: CYAC: Novels in verse. | Swans--Fiction. | Artists--Fiction. |
    Jews--Fiction. | Magic--Fiction. | Courts and courtiers--Fiction. |
    Ludwig II, King of Bavaria, 1845-1886--Fiction. | Bavaria
    (Germany)--History--1777-1918--Fiction. | Fairy tales. | LCGFT: Novels
    in verse. | Fairy tales.
Classification: LCC PZ5.R614 War 2023 | DDC [Fic]--dc23
LC record available at https://lccn.loc.gov/2022056188

# A WARNING ABOUT SWANS

## R. M. ROMERO

PEACHTREE
*Teen*

In memory of
Frank Mendelsohn, z"l

"In olden times, when wishing
still helped . . ."
—The Brothers Grimm

THE **FIRST** TALE

THE DAUGHTER OF AIR

### Prologue

**There are those who say**
I gave
      my heart,
      my body,
      the wisp of my soul
to Baron Maximilian von Richter
for a fistful of diamonds,
a clutch of pearls,
a castle in the Bavarian Alps,
where summer is a myth
and winter an unrelenting tyrant.

But I didn't give up
my woods,
my wings,
my world

for a boy.
I gave them up
for something
far more precious
than a crown or a kiss.

I gave them up
to be *free.*

## Chapter One

**Like the heroine**
in any good story,
I was

      (I *am*)

the youngest
of six sisters.

We were maidens of myth
and children of the air.
Our names were forest lullabies:
Mist and Kara,
Rota and Sigrun and Eir.
And I, Hilde.
Hilde, with a fury of red hair.
Hilde, with magic waiting at her fingertips.

There are many stories
about us.
Less than half are true;
less than half are *real*.

Here is what I know:
we six sisters
were not born, but dreamed by a man
named Odin.

**Chapter Two**

**Odin acquired his magic**
through death.

He told my sisters and me
he chose to die
in the hopes of rising
as something *new*.

Odin hung from an ash tree,
        (its boughs
                twisted
        with age)
his side pierced by a spear,
his right eye open,

his left an empty socket
weeping stardust and blood
in equal amounts.

As Odin died,
he wished,
he writhed,
he *dreamed*.
And magic flowed
from the ash's roots, flooding
his bones.

Some believe
Odin became a god in that moment,
that he stepped down from the ash tree
as the father of all
death and enchantment.

But I think he was only *our* father,
a magician
who wrapped his fingers too tightly
            around the world
                  and *squeezed*.

**When he returned to life,**
Odin was changed,
a man whose powers could withstand
the pull of time itself.

And crowded around him
were the dreams he'd had
while dying:
wolves, ravens, and foxes
leaked from the imagination
stored behind Odin's single eye.

My sisters and I were the only myths
he made who looked
                brittle, small, *human.*

But inside
our girlish limbs and hearts,
we held the same power
our father had learned
at the ash tree:
the ability to bring dreams
to life.

## Chapter Three

**My sisters and I came of age**
in a vast green wood.

Our forest was a secret,
and like all the best secrets,
it was well kept

on the slopes of a steep mountain.
Far from castles, roads, and railways,
we didn't know the world
held anything except joy.

We six
spent each morning
listening to our father's wisdom
as we lolled on beds of soft moss,
our bodies draped in purple blossoms
and the light piercing the trees.

*Choose the dreams*
*you bring into the world*
*with care,* Odin told us.
*Choose only those*
*that deserve to roam the forest floor*
*and soar above it.*
*Choose only those*
*that deserve to be seen*
*and held by others.*

I leaned forward,
my chin cupped in my hands,
my heart and hopes blooming
like the flowers I lay in.
*I can't wait*
*to make my own dreams*
*real!*

But Odin shook his silver head.
Even in those days,
he was weathered by the ages.
*You and your sisters*
*began as dreams.*
*You are wish-maidens—*
*and a wish*
*cannot make a wish of its own.*
*You can only use your magic*
*on behalf of others.*
*So use it*
*wisely.*

My sisters bowed their heads
in acceptance.

                           (I could not.)

**I trailed after Odin**
whenever I could find him
as he traveled through the woods,
my questions falling
like raindrops.

I asked him:
*How will we know*
*which dreams are worthy*
*of being made real?*

I asked him:
*What lies at the foot of the mountain,*
*where our forest meets*
*with a blue, blue lake?*
*I've seen it from the tops*
*of my favorite climbing trees.*

Odin put his hand
on my head.
Against the red flare of my curls,
his fingers were bright and pale
as bone.

*A worthy dream*
*makes the world*
            *(and the woods)*
*kinder,*
*stronger,*
*more beautiful,* he said.
*That is why*
*I dreamed*
*you and your sisters—*
*because the six of you*
*are all those things.*

*As for what is beyond*
*our woods ...*
*It is the world of men.*

*They are beasts*
*I did not make.*
*They carry bullets and arrows*
    *(the bite of each*
      *worse than any adder's)*
*and lie in wait to strike*
*down the innocent.*

*Stay here*
*in the forest, little Hilde.*
*Stay hidden*
*from the world of men*
*and the wickedness in it.*

*Stay here*
*and stay safe.*

## Chapter Four

**As children, our only duty**
to the forest
was to bring the simple dreams
of the woodland creatures
to life.

The animals longed
for summer to last forever,

for a hollow tree to nest safely in,
for their bellies to be filled
with a deer or patch of berries.

My sisters tried their best
to grant these wishes.
But the first dream
*I* conjured from another's mind
wasn't the dream
of an otter or a stag.

I chose
the dream of a little boy.

**My sisters and I found him**
      (human and delicate
      as a single flower petal)
at the outermost edge of our forest;
it was the first time
we'd ever dared to stand on the threshold
of the land of men.

The boy was napping
beneath a solitary beech tree.
His breath whistled as he dozed;
his leather cap had slipped
over his eyes.

Intrigued
       (despite ourselves)
my sisters and I scaled the beech,
giggling
around the taste of the forbidden,
tart and new.
We crouched in the tree's uppermost branches,
staring at the slumbering boy.

*I've never seen*
*a boy before,* Mist whispered,
peering down
at the human child.

*Yes, you have!* argued Kara.
*Odin All-Father is a boy.*

*He is a man, fully grown—*
*like this tree,* Rota pointed out.
This *boy is just a sapling*
*and human at that!*

Sigrun bared her teeth.
*We should chase him away!*
*This beech*
*is at the entrance*
*to our woods!*
*He's too close*

*to straying inside*
*for my liking.*

Eir let out a little cry.
*Don't!*
*We shouldn't do him harm*
*when he's done none*
*to us.*

I ignored
my sisters and their quarrel.
I was fascinated by the dream
curling from the boy's temples
like smoke:
an endless field of sunflowers
stretching
toward the horizon.

I loved its golden light;
it was the color of *life.*
It spoke
of a new melody to be sung,
a new day to dance through.
And the longer
I watched the boy,
the more the magic running through me
called out to be used.

(And used *well.*)

**I slid down the tree**
so quietly
not even my sisters noticed.

I stood over the boy
and moved my hands through the air,
pulling his dream
            (full of tomorrows)
into the world, thread by thread.

It began
as a muted splash of color
in the air.
Then, all at once, flower after flower
opened
in a ring of light
            (never-ending)
around the child.

My work done,
I clambered back up the tree.
And when the boy's eyes fluttered open,
he was surrounded by sunflowers,
warm as an embrace.

I was satisfied
with what I had made ...
and the smile
blossoming on the human boy's lips.

**My sisters didn't appreciate**
what I'd done.
When we returned
to the green heart of the woods
                    (our woods)
the five of them enfolded me,
first with their arms,
then with their words.

One's sister's voice
        bled
into that of the next.
They were a single chain of confusion
                    (and fear)
as they hissed:
*What did you do, Hilde?*
*You shouldn't have gotten*
*so close to the boy!*
*You shouldn't have made*
*his dream real!*

*What if he'd woken up?* asked Sigrun.
*What if he'd had*
*a rifle, a bow, an arrow*
*tucked away*
*in his jacket?*

Kara clicked her tongue at me.
*Our father has warned us*
*about such evil things!*

*He was just a boy,* I insisted.
*And it was just*
*a dream of flowers.*
*Neither one*
*could have hurt us—*
*or anything in the woods.*

Unwilling to hear
more of their worries,
I tossed my head
and left my sisters to their fear.

I was thinking
only of sunflowers.

## Chapter Five

**My first sight of the dangers**
lurking in the great graying world
arrived in the form of a wolf,
a bullet buried in its chest,
deep as heartbreak always is.
Odin and I
waded through
a red sea of autumn leaves
to find the wolf.

We followed the path
laid out by its sunken footprints
and the blood pooled in each until
we discovered the dying thing.

      (My kin, my fellow dream.)


The All-Father knelt beside the wolf,
his eye

      roaming
over the red tangle of its stomach
and the steel lodged in it.
He stroked
the wolf's dark muzzle,
its arched back, its heaving sides.
*I'm sorry*
*this happened to you.*
*But you must leave*
*your body now.*
*You must move on*
*to the Other Wood—*
*the forest that waits for us all*
*at the end of the long,*

        *winding*
*path we call life.*


The wolf whined,
scratching at the dirt,
as if it could still race through the trees
and dive into the shadows
cast by their boughs.

I gritted my teeth against the agony
        (firelight red and just as hot)
flooding the wolf.
*Why* won't *it leave?* I asked Odin.
*It's in*

        *so much*

            *pain.*


Odin lifted his hands
from the wolf's blood-soaked fur.
They came away black,
like the wolf had poured the night
into my father's palms.


*Some souls cannot find their way*
*out of the labyrinth*
*made by the body,* Odin said.
*Not without help*
*from another.*


**A spirit has a weight to it—**
it's heavy
with broken promises,
days never spent in the sun.
A spirit has a texture to it—
like milk and moonlight.

I felt these things
as Odin pulled the wolf's soul
from between the ridges of its teeth,
yellow from all the summers
it had eaten.

I refused to look away,
even as the wolf's heart song
ended—a cord cut.
I refused to cry,
even as the animal
lapsed into
a forever stillness.

> (I *should* have cried;
> I *should* have looked away.
> My steady gaze
> and the absence of tears
> were my undoing.)

Odin held the wolf's spirit
up to the midday sky—an offering, a sacrifice.
*There is a road to the Other Wood*
*laid out by the stars—*
*a path*
*only spirits can tread,* he told me.
*Some of us*
*can see it.*

I squinted upward.
I saw nothing
but the clouds,
ordinary as the slim birch trees.
*Can you see the road, Father?*

*Yes.*
*And because I can,*
*I am able to send souls*
*down that path*
*so they can be at peace.*
Odin opened his hands.
The wolf's soul, a flicker
of firefly-brilliance,
sailed past me into the sun
and the sweetness of the hereafter.

I watched it go,
the ache in my chest
building.
It felt like I had swallowed
a stone.
But I still
        didn't
                cry.

                              (I wish now,
                        more than anything,

I had.
Yet a wish
from a maid like me—
a wish herself—
meant little in the woods.)

**Chapter Six**

**The death I'd witnessed**
changed Odin.
He began to stalk the woods
as the wolf once had,
his gaze so sharp
the deer, the rabbits, the softer creatures
danced away
whenever he approached.

He reminded
my sisters and me daily:
*Never stray*
*from the forest;*
*never venture*
*down to the lake.*

Perhaps Odin was right
to fear for us.

We *were* different
than the other dream creatures.

Our movements
were hindered by our clumsy girl's feet
and fine hair
             (red and gold and black as earth)
that snagged
on branches and brambles.

Mindful of these shortcomings,
our animal cousins
tried to instruct us
in the ways of the forest.

They tried to keep us
alive and well.

**The ravens taught us:**
how to remember a face forever,
how to laugh as we tumbled
down snowbanks and green summer hills.

The foxes taught us:
how to move so quietly
we were mistaken for moonlight,
how to see without being *seen*.

The wolves taught us:
how to throw ourselves into danger,
how to put our teeth to good use.

The patience of our animal cousins was long
as a winter's night.
But their lessons failed
to satisfy Odin,
and we sisters
did not remain as only dream-maidens
         (almost helpless,
         almost prey)
for long.

**At the closing of our ninth summer,**
Odin gave us cloaks of starlight.

He'd woven them
night after sleepless night,
his hands moving faster than the comets
he'd stolen the light from,
his brow furrowed like a ravine.

After the last stitch
had been cinched closed,
Odin placed the cloaks,
white as wintry peaks,
across our laps.

Our father said:
*Whenever you wear these,*
*you will become*
*more than just girls who spin dreams.*
*You will become*
swans
*and carry the beginnings of storms*
*beneath your wings.*

My sisters and I squawked
in delight.
Now we would be equal
to the other beasts;
now we, too, would have claws.

Odin raised his hand,
extinguishing the spark of our joy.
The six of us
       fell
silent as snowfall.

*Each of these cloaks*
*has a different gift*
*stitched into it,* Odin said.
*A gift of magic, a gift of power.*
*And with the gift*
*that is yours*
        *(and yours alone)*

*you will each perform*
*a different duty*
*for the forest.*

*Do that duty well,*
*my children,*
*my daughters of air.*
*Remember: you were made*
*of and for*
*the forest.*

## Chapter Seven

**When Mist wore her cloak,**
she brought life
into the woods.
She planted souls
inside new bodies and stood guard
over each fawn, blue robin's egg,
rose-pink fox kit.

*Aren't they wonderful?*
Mist would ask,
her winter-pale fingers
stroking the heads of the babies.

Kara and Sigrun had been granted
swiftness and strength.
On quicksilver wings,
they taught
the badger cubs and wildcat kittens
to outrace the wind
and fight with all the mercy
of a thunderstorm.

*Come with us!*
Kara and Sigrun would say,
pulling me to my feet,
throwing my feathered cloak
over my shoulders.

(I was never able to keep up.)

Rota could curl her tongue
around any language instantly
and command it
to do her bidding.
She ended wars
between crows and squirrels
before they could even begin;
she bargained
for meat and warm copses of trees
with bears and wolves.

*The trick to learning*
*a new language*
*is to listen,* Rota would tell me,
closing my eyes
with a pass of her hand
so my (dark) world
was made of

       yips,

       howls,

       steady breaths.

And at night,
Eir sang the woods to sleep,
her voice honeybee-sweet
and soaked in magic.

*Fall into shadow,*
*fall into the claws*
*and wings of those*
*who are gone,*
she would whisper
as we sisters lay together,
our heads tucked beneath
the bright expanse of our wings.

**What gift was I given**
by Odin and my starlit cloak?

The gift
       of greeting
            death.

Like Odin before me,
I could coax souls from bodies,
guiding them like a thread
through the eye of a needle.

I tried
to give comfort to dying creatures,
spreading my swan wings
over their broken paws and talons.

(I never flinched
as blood
       seeped
           into
my feathers.)

I showed spirits the long road
winding toward the Other Wood,
a line of silver rising to meet
my fingertips
like a scar.
For I could see now too.

What gift was I given?
A burden ...
and a heavy one at that.

**I envied my sisters;**
they carried their gifts well.
They never resented
the cloaks they wore
or the power
flowing in the twisted threads.

I, however, did.
Night after night,
I was forced to leave our nest,
roused by

>>the last growl of a badger,
>>the final flutter of an owl's wings.

Beneath the eye of the moon

>>(watchful and pale
>>as Odin's own)

I gathered souls
as my sisters gathered blackberries,
the taste of endings
bursting copper-bitter on my tongue.

*I wish you could all live*
*forever,* I told bison and stag,

hawk and sparrow.
But for every life,
there must be a death
and I could save no one.
(Not even myself.)

**The only time silence ever filled my mind**
was when I removed my cloak.

No souls spoke to me
so long as its threads
didn't brush my skin.
It was almost worth
the momentary loss of my wings.

But I had a duty—
to the dead and the forest,
as my sisters reminded me
day after day.

Rota would sigh
       (ever strong, ever practical,
       ever sturdy as an oak)
whenever I complained.
*I know you believe*
*your gift is a curse, Hilde.*
*But without you,*

*lost souls might haunt our forest,*
*until every tree and river*
*was stained silver,*
*until the wind sang only*
*of their loneliness.*

*You don't know*
*what it's like,* I spat.
*To watch your feathers*
*turn red with blood,*
*to breathe in last moments.*

Eir brushed her wings
          (pure, untouched
          by violence)
against my own.
*We all protect the forest*
*in our own ways.*
*And it protects us*
*in return.*
*The woods give us*
*trees to shelter under,*
*rivers to swim in,*
*flowers to braid in our hair.*
*Our part of the world*
*is beautiful—*
*even the mushrooms, even the bones.*

I pulled away from my sisters.
The truth I held inside me
wouldn't be heard
by near-girls, near-swans
who'd never watched the light dim
in another's eyes.

So I swallowed my tales of blood
and darkness
and sought out Odin instead.

## Chapter Eight

**I found Odin**
      (gaunt and thin
        as I felt)
in the gentle melancholy of twilight.
But the questions I asked him
were anything but soft.

*Why did you give me*
*this gift?*
*Did you believe*
*my hands would be steadier*
      *than Eir's*
*when I held souls in them?*

*Did you think*
*my voice would be gentler*
         *than Rota's and Sigrun's*
*when I said my goodbyes?*
*Did you understand*
*my lip would tremble less*
         *than Mist's*
*when I untangled*
*spirits from their rib cages?*

Odin's smile
was tinted by the blue of the dying day.
*I gave you*
*my own gift*
*because I saw you with the wolf.*
*You (alone) never wept*
*when faced with suffering.*
*You (alone) can carry sorrow*
*without being crushed by it.*
*You (alone) did not flee*
*from the sight of death.*
*You may be*
*the youngest, Hilde,*
*but you are also*
*the strongest*
*in ways even I*
*did not intend.*

(If only
I could have wrung tears from my eyes
on the day the wolf departed
for the Other Wood!
The wolf deserved them—
and I deserved
the joy
of my childhood *back*.)

I shook my head.
*I don't feel strong.*
*I only feel tired.*

Odin leaned against an oak;
it bore his weight, his years
without complaint.
*Come with me, Hilde.*
*I have a story to tell you.*
*One your sisters*
*need not hear.*

**I knew the place Odin led me to**
for what it is:
a boneyard, a haunt.

Gray and faceless stones
jutted from the lichen,
marking the graves of the creatures
buried there.

Who were they?
Who might they *still* be
in another world
colored by nothing
but the rain?

I circled the stones,
counting them off
on my fingers;
there were six in all.

Odin stretched
a withered hand
out across the nearest stone.
*You are a new creature, Hilde.*
*But your power*
*is ancient.*
*Once, there were more of us*
*who saw the silver road.*

*We traveled*
*through woods and vales,*
*collecting spirits, sending them on.*
*The names of the others were:*
*Holda, Berchtold, and Krampus,*
*Perchta, Rübezahl, and Hel.*
*We called ourselves*
the Wild Hunt, *for we*
*were untamed.*

I wanted to carve
the names of the Wild Hunt in me,
these former members
of our brotherhood, our sisterhood.
*They should be here*
*with us now!*

Odin raised his head,
watching the daylight
turn into a ghost of itself.
*No enchantment*
*can persist forever, Hilde.*
*Magic is a river*
*that will eventually run dry*
*for us all.*
*Their magic waned—*
*and so did they.*

I didn't realize
every word
our father spoke that day
was said in farewell.

**Odin disappeared when we were ten.**
It's been six years
since any creature saw him—
my sisters and I included.

Did he grow tired of our woods?
Did he leave to weave
new dreams in distant lands?
Or did he fade away
        (as most creatures believe),
his magic no more
than one last sigh on the wind?
        (As he said
            *all* magic would be, someday.)


Whatever became of Odin.
I don't expect
we'll ever see him again.
Why would we?
He had done his duty
as our father, arming us
                (and the forest)
against the threats
he worried we might one day face.

But it stings
like a fistful of nettles to know
he didn't say goodbye.

## Chapter Nine

In the wake of the All-Father's absence,
I tried to be obedient
and hide
my growing discontent
in the earth alongside
the empty bones.

I tried to live,
even if my charges
could not.
And in the rare moments
when life reigned
and death didn't creep
into the woods,
I joined my sisters, seeking happiness
in how we brought
the uncomplicated dreams
of the forest animals to life.

We planted new vales of flowers
for the deer;
we opened the sky's doors
for the otters,
drawing rain from the clouds.

But this happiness
was interrupted
                    (time and time again)
by a creature's
            last
                    gasp,
and I had to leave my sisters
to answer
the calls of the dying.

My gift was a stone
tied to my ankle,
pinning me down.
It cast me
out of the circle of laughter
        (bright as the sunflowers
        springing from a boy's imagination)
my sisters formed.

I wanted
someone to understand me
as my sisters could not;
I wanted
a Wild Hunt of my own,
brethren to fly with me
and share
the sight of the silver road
and the heaviness of souls.

I *wanted.*

But I was alone, pieced together
from only my longings.

**When I was thirteen, I asked a crow**
about love.

Of all my animal siblings,
the crows were the only ones
who didn't change partners
with the seasons,
abandoning them to winter
in favor
of a new spring love.

When crows chose each other,
they chose *forever.*

My sisters believed
the crows were too sentimental,
with their funerals,
their dances,
their memories longer
than any stream.

But I admired their devotion
to both their grudges
and those they loved.

And of all the dream creatures,
the crows
were most like me.
They, too,
saw the road in the sky.

If anything could teach me
how to live with death and joy,
I believed
it would be the crows.

**The crow I sought out**
made her home
in the eastern part of the forest.

I waited until her mate
had gone in search of carrion;
I wanted privacy
for this conversation.

I climbed her pine tree,
branch
by branch,
step
by step,
moving slowly.
The crow had eggs to tend to

and I was less threatening as a girl
than a swan.

As I reached the final branch,
I nodded at the crow.

She nodded back, accepting
my presence.
*You came to ask me*
*a question,*
*not-a-swan, not-a-girl.*
*I see it wriggling*
*on your tongue.*
*Well?*
*What is it?*

*How did you choose*
*your forever-companion?* I asked.
*What made him more special*
*than all the other crows?*

The crow laughed.
With me—
         or at me?
It was impossible to tell
with corvids.
*Why, not-a-swan?*
*Why, not-a-girl?*

*Because my mate*
*knows the best dances,*
*the best hills to roll down*
*when it snows.*
*Because when a storm*
*shattered my wing,*
*he did not leave me*
*to the wolves,*
*even though I was broken.*
*Because he and I*
*move as one*
*whenever we fly.*

I shifted
further along the branch,
coming close enough
for my whispers to be heard,
staying far enough
from the nest that I couldn't reach
the crow's eggs.

      (As the keeper
      of too many endings,
      they were a beginning
      I envied.)

*How will I know*
*when I want to spend forever*
*with another?*
*How can I find a creature*

*who won't make me feel as alone*
*as I do now?*

The crow shook the dew
from her wings.
*Because the other will speak*
*the language of your body—*
*how to touch you*
*and be touched by you.*
*They will know the right jokes*
*to pull laughter*
*from your belly.*
*And because*
*you will want*
*to run from them.*

I blinked, a trick
I'd learned from the owls.
*Why would I run?*

If the crow
could have smiled then,
she would have.
*Your loneliness may be*
*a black pit,*
*threatening to eat you*
*alive.*
*But it is even more terrifying*

*to be understood*
*by anything outside*
*your own reckless heart.*

I didn't know what to make
of the crow's warning then;
But I carried it with me ...
even many years later.

## Chapter Ten

**I was sixteen and rising**
when I gave up
    my old life,
    my sisters,
    the forest,
    the creatures tucked away
    in the pines and the beeches.

What drove me from the forest
on a bright spring day?
It wasn't my discontent, my resentment,
the bottomless well of my loneliness.

It was the shriek of a hawk
in the world of men,

where the last trees of our wood
joined with the far side
of the lake.

I almost never heard
the cries of the dying
echoing
outside the borders of our forest.
But the hawk's shriek
rattled,
        desperate,
in my mind.

*I am so ready*
*to leave,* the hawk moaned.
*I am so ready*
*to step out of this*
*(broken) body.*
*But I cannot find the way.*

I turned
toward the lake and the hawk,
opening
my wings for both.
I flew onward . . .
        without ever
           looking back.

**I touched down**
       (Hilde, alone)
on the blue waters of the lake
and drifted to the other side
       (so far from my woods)
on my white belly.

But there was no time to marvel
at the lake—
how enormous it was,
how cool the water felt
on both feathers and skin,
how the yew trees here did not belong
to my childhood forest.

The hawk lying on the bank
pulled me to it
with more urgency
than the current.

An arrow
pierced its heart, breaking it
as mine had broken so often
in the woods.
The hawk
would never soar again
or scrub the tears
from its black eyes.

Gently, I untangled its soul
from the net of muscle and skin
holding it captive
and lifted it to the sky.
And as its spirit
left the world, unburdened by pain,
I let my cloak
roll off my shoulders,
taking my wings and my swan self
with it.

I didn't want to hear
more spirits that day ...
and I had yet to notice
I was being watched
by a boy half hidden
in the shadow of a yew tree.

**Chapter Eleven**

**Odin was the *only* man**
I'd ever met.
His face had been scarred
by all the strange things
        (and monsters)
he'd seen and created.

R. M. Romero

But the boy beside the lake
was *handsome*.

His features were made to be captured
in the pages of history.
His profile was strong,
his eyes dark pools
much deeper than any river
I'd dipped into.
He wore leather trousers
embroidered with pale alpine flowers.
A jaunty hat perched on his head
like a bird.

*Are you
a fairy?* the boy asked.

**I started, struck by the words,**
as my wings
had once been struck by lightning.

*I'm a girl,* I (half) lied.

*But a moment ago,
you were a swan.*
The boy's honesty
was a knife;
it cut easily through my falsehoods.

Still, I was quick to tell him:
*I don't know what you mean.*
*I've always been a girl.*

The boy jumped to his feet.
His boots left scars
in the mud.
*I saw you—*
*I saw the real you.*
*I've waited my entire life*
            *(eighteen whole years!)*
*to see something like you.*
*My father*
*warned me about swans.*
*He said*
*they can be vicious—*
*that they were made to break*
*rather than be broken.*
*But you*
*are extraordinary.*

The boy smiled at me.
*Will you show me?*
*Will you show me*
*how you fly?*
*Please?*

The sharpness of his grin
might have alarmed
another girl.
But to me, it was familiar;
wolves wear the same smile
when they see something
they hunger for.

And this boy
was as hungry for wonder
as I was for company
whose heart still roared with life.

I knew his longing
       (for more, for *better*)
too well
to dismiss him.

**I donned my cloak again ...**
slowly.

The moment
it slid
over my body,
my skin prickled,
feathers freeing themselves from it.
My arms and neck
lengthened, turning first-frost white.

I tucked my legs
against the swell of my stomach
and spread my wings.

I flew so high
I imagined
the tips of my wings
scraped the stars
and the silver path
winding around them.

      (There is so much freedom
            in refusing
                  to touch the ground.)

**I circled**
the mirror-still lake once
before landing
on its surface again.
My white cloak slipped down
around my waist,
like I'd stolen a stray wisp of cloud.

The boy stared
as I waded back to shore,
      tilting
his head to the side,
the gesture more lynx

than human.
*That was beautiful,* he whispered.
You're *beautiful!*

My cheeks flushed.
I didn't know
how to accept a compliment
about my nature;
I was
what I was.

(Odin had made certain
of *that*.)

*You don't seem surprised
by any of this,* I said.
*Why?
You're human!*

The boy lifted his head
to the yew boughs above.
*I've always seen the world
stripped to its bones
like a tree in winter,
and my father fed me
enough fairy tales
for me to know the truth.
It is in the magic
every time.*

**I asked the boy:**
*What's your name?*

I wanted to be the first one
*to* ask.
I knew the power of holding a name
      (a true name)
on the tip of my tongue.

*Baron Maximilian von Richter,* he said.
*But you may call me* Richter,
*if you like.*
*And your name is . . . ?*

What name to offer him?
The one
in the muted language of flowers,
in the whispered tongues of foxes,
in the low grumblings of boars,
in the hollow rattling of the dead?

Only the name Odin had given me
would do.
*Hilde.*
*My name is Hilde.*

*Hilde,* Richter sighed.
*That's lovely.*
*Like the name of a queen.*

I tucked my hair behind my ears
the way Kara did
when she combed it with swift fingers.
*I'm not a queen.*
*I'm like everything else*
*that lives and dies*
*in my forest.*

*Oh, Hilde.*
Richter's grin was a waxing moon,
growing wider, *brighter*
with each moment.
*You're like nothing else*
*living* anywhere.

## Chapter Twelve

**I returned to the lake**
and the land of men
every morning after
for seven days.

Richter was always there,
waiting.
He shared his meals

      (beets and potatoes,
      *Dampfnudeln* pastries,
      plump strawberries
      shaped like our hearts)
and his life
with me.

Every story the boy told
sounded like a thread
being pulled taut
against his throat ...
and his future.
In a way, they mirrored
my own.

*My ancestors were knights,*
*rumored to slay dragons*
*with their golden swords,* Richter said.
*My own father was a baron*
*and a great favorite*
*of King Ludwig.*
*He swore*
*our family would one day rule*
*all of Bavaria.*

*Bavaria?* I asked.
*What is that?*
The name was foreign to me.

No birds
had whistled it in my ear,
no fish
spelled it with their tails
in the streams.

*This land.*
*This kingdom.*
*This place*
*we're in right now.*
Richter laughed.
*I suppose*
*that's a very human idea—*
*naming everything we touch,*
*placing borders*
*on the world.*

**Richter sighed then,**
his shadow
creeping
toward mine as dusk spread
its phoenix-fire over the lake.

(Had I really spent
the entire day beside him?
Time had moved so quickly
in the presence of a friend.)

*My father*
*died not long ago,* Richter murmured.
*Despite his vows, he left me*
*nothing but his debts.*
*Now I live in a castle*
*that feels like it, too,*
*is dying.*
*I can't stand being there,*
*confined to its crumbling halls—*
*to the cage*
*my life has become.*

*So I wander*
*to the lake, the town,*
*to the places that whisper*
*about what my future could be.*
*If only*
*I had the power to seize it!*

> (Like a magician.
> Like Odin.
> Like someone who deals in more
> than death.)

**I reached for Richter then,**
closing my hand around his.
He was so warm,
summer
in the shape of a boy.

*I know*
*what it's like to feel trapped*
*in your own home,* I told him.
*My sisters are content*
*with the lives our father gave us.*
*But I can't be.*

*I still envy you.*
Richter's smile
hung uneasily from his mouth,
a broken wing
never to be mended.
*You have companionship.*
*And I*
*am almost always*
*alone.*

I threaded a hand
through my hair,
trying to tame the blaze in me.
*I feel more alone*
*beside my sisters*
*than I ever do*
*when I'm away from them.*

Richter raised a brow.
*Do you feel alone now?*
*Here, with me?*

I smiled and said,
*Less so*
*than usual.*

**Chapter Thirteen**

**What I learned from the boy beside the lake:**

How to dance a Viennese waltz
on the bankside,
how to let him lead me
through the steps until we were
winded and laughing.

How to name
the world around me
with a human tongue,
from Lake Forggensee to the town of Füssen
to the great city of Munich.

How to forget who I am
and where I come from.

**I showed Richter moments of magic,**
weaving dreams
of crisp apples and warm dens

for voles and mice,
and laying out
the whole of my life
      (and my cloak)
on the lakeshore
for him.

We sat back-to-back,
Richter's shoulders
pressing against mine.
      (Wingless and empty.)
I felt how anchored he was
to the ground, the lake, the moment.
The boy was not
a son of air
like me and my sisters;
he was all earth.

My own stories felt quaint
compared to all the places
Richter spoke about.
But he ate up my tales eagerly
with his bread and butter.

*My sisters*
*teach blue jays to fly*
*and foxes to run.*
*They drive*

*vultures from the beeches*
*and blizzards*
*from the sky with the beat*
*of their wings.*

*And I take souls and send them*
*into the wind.*
*But I've never seen*
*a city,*
*never walked paths*
*shaped by more than deer.*
*My life is so small*
*it was held*
*inside my father's dreams.*

***Your duty to your woods***
*is a difficult one,* Richter said.
*I don't know anyone else*
*who could shoulder it.*
*In the human world,*
*there are no girls like you.*
　　　　*(Half a bird,*
　　　　　*half something else.)*

*But there are girls*
*who lead armies to victory,*
*whose ink-stained fingers*
*pen fantastical stories,*

*who dance like snowflakes*
*for hundreds to see.*

*In the human world,*
*none of us were born for a purpose.*
*None of us exist*
*in the confines of someone else's dream,*
*to be forgotten upon waking.*

*In the human world, we can choose*
*the forms*
*our own lives take.*

I closed my eyes and imagined
dancing on light feet,
not weighed down by a single soul
that wasn't my own.

I imagined
laughing with friends like Richter,
uninterrupted by the moan of spirits.

I imagined
being human.

(Or close to it.)

*Without your cloak,*
would *you be human,*
*just like I am?*
Richter asked suddenly.
*Would your magic*
*fade like the mist does*
*each morning over this lake?*

I could have lied.
I could have told Richter
every drop of my magic
was locked in the starlit seams.

                    I didn't.

This boy had been open
about his own truths,
and a friendship
            (my first)
can never survive
on lies.

I told him:
*Without the cloak,*
*I can't turn*
            *(back)*
*into a swan.*
*I can't hear souls*

*and free them*
*from their unquiet bones.*
*My cloak, my wings, the silver road*
*are a part of me now—*
*whether I want these gifts*
*or not.*

*But with or without it*
            *(and my wings),*
*I can still make dreams*
*real.*
*And I will live much longer*
*than any human girl.*
*I can't change*
*what I was born as—*
*a wish-maiden*
*down to the marrow.*
*There is no escaping*
*the magic in me.*

## Chapter Fourteen

**I arrived at the lake**
on the eighth morning ...
but Richter was not there.

I paced
on the bank, wondering
if he'd grown tired of our conversations
and the longing tinting them
lupine purple.
Maybe my adventure with the boy
who ached for magic
was finally at an end.

I was about to abandon the lake
and fly back
to the woods, the lost souls, my sisters
when Richter
burst from the trees.
He held his side;
I could almost feel
the stitch forming there,
a lesser version
of Odin's old wound.

*Hilde!* Richter gasped.
The light in his eyes
was wild,
a star
on the verge of its last dance.
*I found an injured boar*
*in a strawberry patch*
*not far from here.*

*Can you help it?*
*It's in so much pain!*

*I can try,* I told him.

Richter gave me a nod—and a promise.
*I'll come with you.*

My breath
snagged in my throat
as my fingers had snagged
on blackthorn before.
My sisters
never offered to follow
the final murmur of a heart
with me.
But this human boy *had.*

*Thank you,* I said to Richter,
and slipped my cloak on.
The instant I did,
I heard
the mournful bellow of the boar—
its cry so much louder
than the wail
of my own thoughts.

Richter and I
      (boy and swan)
dove into the trees
to find it.

**The boar lying in the strawberry patch**
was already dying,
like the wolf, like hundreds of others
before it.

The arrow
jutting from its red belly
told me a hunter had been here ...
and vanished into nothing
but memory.
(As specters always do.)

I was
      (I am)
not like Eir
      (my fifth sister)
who knows the sweetest lullabies.
But I could still
wrap my wings around the boar
and whisper to it
in the language
of the birches and alders,

soft and silver
as the path
its soul would soon wander.

*It's calm*
*where you are going.*
*It's bright*
*where you are going.*
*So be still*
*with me.*
*The Other Wood*
*is waiting for you.*

The boar's soul
looked like a vine
curling from the soil
as I eased it out of its skin
and up
to the flawless spring sky.

Richter watched, as unblinking
as any mortal can be.
The sight of a spirit
undressed from its bones
was almost a miracle,
even to a boy
born into a fairy-tale bloodline.

I sat with the boar's body after,
  digging
      my claws
into the strawberries.
I let myself go cold;
I let the berries weep
when I couldn't.
I was used to welcoming death ...
but I never met it
with a smile.

                    (That was the last time
                        I touched a soul.
                      Maybe it will be
                          the last time
                          I ever do.)


**Alone with the dead**
and the boy
      (both bleeding out
      desperate dreams)
my thoughts
filled with visions of my lively sisters.

They found peace in
      the soft moss under their feet,
      the sight of snug rabbit warrens,
      the song of the larks.

But they had not been called
by the Other Wood;
they were not the sole member
of the Wild Hunt,
the spirits they carried
crushing their own.
Only I
had to face that darkness.

If I lived
in the human world,
if I were a girl
who waltzed in satin shoes
rather than one running
river-wild,
souls and sobs caught
in the breeze around me,
could I find the peace
Odin's gift had stolen from me?

By abandoning
my wings and my duty,
could I be
more than my loneliness,
more than Odin's forgotten creation?
Could I finally
      be

          happy?

I tore
the cloak from my shoulders
and I stood,
a girl once more.

### Chapter Fifteen

**Richter carried my cloak as he and I**
       (boy and girl, nothing
       more and nothing
       less)
walked back to the lake, our steps
mountain-heavy.

When I reached
the water's edge, Richter offered me
my cloak again.
He began:
*Hilde ...*

I stared at the cloak.
To accept my wings again
would be to reenter a life
where I held death
more closely than any friend.

To refuse my wings
and the (unwanted)
power in the starlight
would be to set off
on a new path.

I met
Richter's gaze,
the steel of it, the sharpness.

He was not the forever-companion
the crow had spoken of,
home in the heart of another.
But he *was* a friend
and I believed he could be
the key to unlocking a door
that would lead me far from the woods—
and the silver road.
And I believed I could be
the same for him.

I chose.

*Will you let me come to the human world*
*with you?* I asked Richter.
*Will you show me Bavaria,*
*the cobblestone streets and the kings?*
*Do you think if I became*

*more girl than bird,*
*more girl than a half-lost story,*
*you and I could throw away*
*the burdens our fathers gave us*
*and make*
*new lives for ourselves?*

*Yes!*
Richter gasped,
my cloak escaping
his fingers.
*Oh yes, Hilde.*
*I have nothing now*
*except my dreams,*
*and they can take the two of us*
*no further*
*than this lake.*
*But if you make those dreams real,*
*we can both be*
*whoever we can imagine ourselves*
*and our tomorrows as . . . together.*

*Then teach me*
*to walk in your world,* I said.
*Teach me to be human.*
*And in exchange,*
*I'll bring your dreams*
*to life.*

In the woods,
a bargain between two creatures
must be sealed in blood.
But one made between friends
requires only faith
and a promise.

It was a promise
Richter extended—
along with his hand.
*Yes. I will help you …*
*and you will help me.*

I took the boy's hand;
I took back my future.

I would be
my own creature,
my own *girl*,
not a pinprick of magic
in someone else's sky,
not a scythe used to sever
a spirit from its bones.

I owed Odin nothing
but my unhappiness.
And now
(I hoped)
that, too,
had come to an end.

## Chapter Sixteen

**Richter's castle was a vulture**
hunched
at the foot of a hill.

The castle's façade was haggard.
Its turrets
pierced the mist like spears;
its windows were dark
and dusty.
I'd never seen anything
so enormous
that was not a mountain peak.

A serpentine road
wound up to a great wooden door.
Richter and I followed it,
careful not to trip

over the many missing stones,
worn smooth by rain
and the centuries,
held together by weeds.


Entering the castle
was like walking into the mouth
of a monster.
Everything around me
      (chipped stone walls,
      dimly lit hallways,
      tapestries woven from ancient threads
      and the dust
      of Richter's forefathers)
was gray,
decaying,
*cold*.


Yet whenever
I brushed against the walls,
I felt a hint of old magic,
growing like ivy, thick and green.
It might have been
what kept the ramparts from buckling,
the roof from caving in,
the colored glass in the little chapel
from cracking.

*Was your father a witch?* I asked.
*There are enchantments here*
*that go deep.*

Richter shook his head.
*If there was ever true magic*
*in this place,*
*it's a ghost of itself these days.*

I nodded.
I understood why Richter
hated his home and sought solace
        (and strength)
elsewhere.
There was none to be had
in the castle.

A ghost
can comfort no one—
not even themself.

**The two of us sat down**
at a long wooden table
in a hall made for feasting.

Here, Richter's losses
        (a mother and father,
        a parade of servants,

the glory of his knightly ancestors)
were palpable, a hole in the world
I could run my fingers along.

(Hadn't Odin
left a similar one
in me?)

Richter gave me beer and hard cheese,
sausage I wouldn't touch
after the boar
in the strawberry patch.

I drove
my fingers into my cloak,
(draped across my lap)
and tried not to think of the nameless,
faceless
hunter
who had brought that boar down.

I could have left my cloak
by the lake and buried
my old self
under the yew trees.
But how
could I simply abandon it?
For all the sorrow

it had brought me,
my cloak was the only thing
I could call my own.
        (For the moment.)

Richter himself touched nothing
on the table.
He watched me as I ate, saying,
*If you learn not to carry*
*the woods in your eyes,*
*no one will ever know*
*what you are, Hilde.*
*You will be human*
*to everyone you meet.*
*We could say you are*
        *an exiled princess from France,*
        *an heiress from America,*
        *a margravine from a line so lost*
        *(and noble)*
        *no one can trace its origin.*
*We could say you are*
*anything and everything.*
*Because that is what*
*you have the potential*
*to be.*

Richter unveiled another smile;
I returned the grin.

Even without my wings,
I still felt ready to take flight
and I loosened my grip (little by little)
on the cloak.

**The bedroom I claimed in the castle**
was pieced together from stones
and silence.

I folded my cloak
and placed it
at the back of the wardrobe

       yawning

       open

in the furthest corner of the room.
I shut the doors, turning
from the muted glow of the starlight
sneaking through
its oak panels.
I behaved
like a (human) girl.

       (Or so I hoped.)

The bed was empty
save for its dusty finery—
the velvet curtains,
the sheets that hadn't been slept in
for years.

No sisters giggled beside me;
no elbows or talons
dug into my arms
as I settled down for the night.

But no souls
asked to be guided
to the road in the stars either.
I was chased into sleep
by exhaustion alone.

## Chapter Seventeen

**Dawn was only a red hint**
on the horizon
when Richter threw open the door
to my (borrowed) room,
whistling a song
I hoped to one day learn.

*I've found*
*a new dress for you*
*among my mother's old things,* said Richter.
*Why don't we start*
*our new lives*
*today?*

I tossed aside
my sheets and my weariness,
the warmth of my smile
matching the rising sun.
*Let's begin.*

**The dreams I turned to reality for Richter**
on my first morning in the castle
were practical.

The boy stretched himself
across the dining hall's cool stones,
closed his eyes ...
and dreamed:
his purse heavy with gold marks,
sapphires falling from his eyes
in place of tears.

He dreamed
fields of rubies red as poppies,
fistfuls of pearls,
a diadem fashioned from the strange universe
living inside him.

And I
brought each into the world.

Starved for beauty, the castle gorged itself
on the gold that rushed like sunlight
through Richter's open palms
when he woke.

*Every story is true,* he whispered
        like a boy
        at prayer.
*Every fairy tale is real.*
*And magic*
        *belongs*
                *to us.*

**As the green of spring deepened,**
Richter taught me
how to be human.

The best of these lessons
were stories about other girls.
The castle library was as thick with them
as it was with dust.

Richter read me
tales about girls
who wore the sun and the moon,
who outfoxed witches,
who wandered in frozen fields,
        barefoot and bloodied,
in search of lost friends.

*You could be*
*any one of these girls,*
he murmured to me
in a voice
quiet as the turn of the pages.

When we'd exhausted his books,
Richter played piano for me,
songs that needed no words
to sound like rainfall or heartbreak.

He instructed me
on how to walk, run, dance
in slow circles
as if my feet had never left
the ground.

Our hands linked, Richter told me:
*I'm giving you roots*
*to the human world, Hilde.*
*And they're roots that won't rot*
*or break.*
*They're eternal.*
*Just*
          *like*
*you.*

## Chapter Eighteen

Now summer roars around the castle,
a poorly tamed beast
burning skin
and stealing the softness from the hills.
I fall into my bed
each night, exhausted
from spinning
Richter's wishes into jewels,
from learning new waltzes
that leave my feet aching.

Tired as I am, I don't sleep
easily.
I'm too excited
for what the next day will bring us—
and the next.

Richter must be too.
He comes to me
one midsummer morning,
smiling, laughing
      (as always)
his fingers wrapped in sapphires.

*(The color of these jewels*
*reminds me of Lake Forggensee,*
*where you changed*
*my life, my destiny,*
*all my tomorrows,*
Richter once told me.

He's worn nothing but sapphires
ever since.)

Richter throws open his arms
        (wide as my wings)
and announces:
*It's time!*
*We are going*
*to the city of Munich,*
*to the palace,*
        *the Munich Residenz,*
*where King Ludwig*
*and the most powerful people*
*in Bavaria live.*
*You'll join the human world—*
*and so will I.*

Despite the crushing heat,
I grin at Richter.
I was a creature of endings,
final moments, last words.

I was not made
for a life of *beginnings*.

But now, in Munich,
I can be.

# THE SECOND TALE

## THE ARTIST IN THE GARDEN

### Chapter Nineteen

**Richter insists**
I wear the latest fashions to Munich,
that I pretend to be
the most stylish of girls.

He dreams me
velvet that runs like a midnight sky
down the length of my body,
satin the color of sun-showers.

But every yard of fabric,
no matter how delicate,
chafes at my skin.
I feel
like an instrument,
my ribs
strings waiting to be played.

*Human beings*
*listen to beauty,* Richter says.
*We make way for it;*
*we value it.*
*Beauty is power,*
*so you must be beautiful*
*to etch your own story*
*into the world.*

I lift
one corner of my newest dress,
wrinkling my nose.
Richter stole
the red of a hundred roses
to make it.
*I feel like a bauble,*
*like a flower*
*in someone else's garden,* I say.
*Is this really beauty?*
*Is this really*
*what I must do to be*
*a girl?*

*Yes,* says Richter,
adjusting the cravat
wrapped around his neck.
Like everything he wears,
it compresses

all his soft places.
*We all must play our parts—*
*in the beginning, at least.*
*The more power we have,*
*the more we can do*
*as we please.*

The magic in me hisses:
*This will not make you happy.*
*Be as you always were.*
*Cast your silk shoes aside,*
*dig your hands*
*into the rain-soaked earth*
*and sing nightingale lullabies.*

The girl in me says:
*Isn't the pinch of too-tight shoes*
*better than blood*
*caked in your feathers,*
*unshed tears lodged in your throat?*
*Make yourself*
*a place all your own*
*in Munich,*
*extend yourself*
*across castles and courtyards.*
*This boy is a dreamer*
*as your sisters were not.*

I am both creatures.

I am neither.

I am torn in two.

But I choose the girl

and leave

my cloak in the wardrobe,

hoping my absence will lull

its magic

to sleep.

## Chapter Twenty

**We do not travel to Munich**
on foot or by horse;
we go by steam engine.

The train crawls like a spider
down into the valley
far below.
It scuttles across steel rails
that could be the spines of giants
felled by the ancient knights
of Richter's family.

Odin's warnings
and Richter's tales
haven't prepared me for

the burn of iron in my nose,

the shimmering heat from the boiler,

the steam from the towering smokestacks,

the clusters of human beings

in the seats beside us,

all smiles, silk, and velvet.

I press
my hands against the windows,
watching the castle, the mountain, the woods
        (our homes and our cages)
blur into streams of color
as they fall further
and further behind us.

I never imagined
anything like this was possible;
I never dared to.

Richter leans in to me.
*They say one day,*
*someone will build a steam engine*
*capable of flying.*
*They say one day,*
*someone will take us*
*all the way to the moon and back.*

I try to imagine
a steam engine rolling across
the silver road
to the Other Wood,
faster than any eagle.

But that road
has faded for me now;
I can barely make out
its shape among the clouds.
If I try hard enough,
      (if I am
        girl enough)
it may soon be no more
than a healed scar, invisible
to the eye
      (if not the heart).

**Munich grows towers, houses, and churches**
as the north side of trees
grows evening shadows and moss.

The Marienplatz at the center of the city
is a vale of flowers.
They fall from the windows
of the New Town Hall,
a torrent of dusky pink.
They form pools

at the bases of marble women,
granite demons who cackle like crows,
iron knights raising the Bavarian flag
       (blue and white
         a mirror of the sky and mountain).

Nothing stands taller in Munich
than the Frauenkirche.
This cathedral
is a most practical heart.
Not even the perpetual wind
       (conjured by a demon—
        or by rumors of one.
        Who can say
        which is true?)
can move its bricks and stones.

I stumble through clouds
of sugar-dusted children holding pastries,
women and men strolling down avenues
wider than any beech's trunk,
wanting this city to fill me
like the richest of meals.

*Every building here*
*is a mountain,* I gasp at Richter.
*Every street is a world!*

*And that is why*
*I brought you here,* he replies.
*Munich is an old city;*
*it holds a thousand years inside its gates—*
*and a thousand stories, too.*
*I hope it can be the home*
*we both want.*

**But our homes and histories**
have a way of following us.

I hear
my sisters in the Marienplatz
before I see them,
their swan song rising
over the roar
of human blood and breath.

>        (The myths are right:
>        swans only sing
>        when we're desperate.
>        The myths are wrong:
>        we have more than one song
>        to free from inside us.)

Rota asks the pigeons:
*Have you seen a human girl*
*who is not a girl?*

Sigrun and Kara beat their wings
against the statues and say:
*Maybe she refuses*
*to blink.*

Eir lays more clues
about who I am
        (who I was)
like bread crumbs
for the other birds.
*Maybe she dances*
*like she is trying to fly,*
*like she's forgotten*
*how to.*

*Please, do you know*
*where she is?* Mist begs.

I want
to call out to my sisters
so Rota can lecture me from now
till the first snowfall,
so Sigrun and Kara
can peck at my hair
in disapproval.

But I want to hide
even more.

The circle made by my sisters
is complete without me
darkening its borders.

**Richter doesn't know the language of swans.**
Latin and German,
French and English are what rolls
off his tongue.

But my sisters sparkle
as they sail around the Marienplatz,
and he knows enchantment
when he sees it.

*Kiss me,* Richter says—
half plea,
half command,
all nonsense.

*Why?*
My voice
        breaks
like glass underfoot;
it's too sharp
for its own good.
        (The way I am,
        the way I wish
        I wasn't.)

Richter's cheek
grazes mine.
*Because your sisters wouldn't.*
*Because a crow,*
*a swan, a snow finch wouldn't.*
*If you want to stay*
                    *(with me)*
*a kiss will make you*
*unrecognizable to them—*
*and more human*
*than ever.*


**I've never thought about kissing Richter,**
never traced the curve of his lips
in my mind,
never wanted our bodies
to collide.


And that is how I know
his plan will work.
It will make me
look like someone else.
It will make me
look *human.*


I don't wait for Richter.
I want
this act, this choice, this *instant*
to be mine.

I crush my mouth against his
like I mean to take his throat
in my teeth.
Richter's own kiss is equally fierce,
burning
like black frost.

When I untangle
myself from Richter,
my swan sisters in bridal white
are gone.

### Chapter Twenty-One

**The city of Munich lived and breathed,**
inhaling the music
falling from lips and accordions,
exhaling the perfume of flowers.

But the Munich Residenz,
the palace of Bavaria's king,
has no soul.
I hate it
the moment Richter and I step inside.

We pass through
ornate rooms that feel hollow.
There is silver
where there should be sunlight,
solemnity
where there should be camaraderie.

Yet we turn the heads
of all those around us.
We are everything
this place envies—
young and wealthy, beautiful and strong.

Richter goes from one well-dressed lord
          (drenched in gold)
to another.
He instantly collects
promise after promise,
friend after friend,
like one of my raven brothers.

The courtiers are no less dazzled
by Richter's grin than they are
by the enormous sapphire
clinging to his ring finger
like a single drop of rain.

(Richter was right:
his jewels are keys.
One look at them
and every door opens.)

The men and women here
are like doves;
they coo and surround us
with their words
and avid eyes.

*(You have been wasted*
*tucked away in the mountains,*
*Baron von Richter!*

*You invested*
*in a railroad?*
*Well, I can see*
*your investments*
*have paid off handsomely!*

*Your companion is lovely!*
*She's from France?*
*Ah yes!*
*There is something*
*so fascinating*
*about the woodland green*
*of her eyes!)*

I smile, unsure
what to say.
I've never been the author
of my own story,
only the one who repeats it.

And I'm still learning
the right words to my new tale.

## Chapter Twenty-Two

**Evening soon falls**
and Richter sweeps me into the ballroom,
notching me against his hip
like a hunting knife.

The click of my heels
on the marble
and the bellowing conversations
of dukes and duchesses
are all too loud.
I want to cup my hands
around my ears and retreat
into the silence
offered by the night.

Instead, I breathe out
     s l o w l y
and look up, seeking
the comforts of the sky.

I am met with only the ceiling.
Yet there are women
with rose-gold wings painted on it,
none of them quite human.
Their smiles are not dark-forest grim
like mine.
These women are pink and new—
mothers and makers,
always beginning, never ending.
Eternity sticks to them
like a briar.

I point and ask Richter,
*Who are they?*

*Saints.*
*Angels.*
*Legends,* he replies.
*Most of us pray to them,*
*begging for favors.*
*But you and I both know*
*you don't get real magic*
*by getting down on your knees.*

I think of Odin
        (not holy,
        just mythic)
pinned to his ash tree
above the forest floor.
*No,* I murmur.
*You don't.*

**Eager to meet the ladies**
floating across the ballroom
        (bright as the mirrors
        lining the walls)
I break free from Richter.

I go to each girl,
introducing myself
with a flutter of white skirts and lashes.

*What have you chosen*
*to do with your life?* I ask,
holding my hands out to them.
I want to collect their answers
as Richter collects his diamonds,
as I collected wildflowers
in the woods of my childhood—
before my gift,
before the dead.
*Are you going to build a steam engine*

*to take you to the stars?*
*Are you writing a story*
*soon to be heard across the world?*
*Tell me, please.*

The girls only stare;
some even giggle
behind their feathered fans.
       (The closest to wings
       they will ever have.)
The answers
they give me are all variations of
       the exact
           same one.
*I'm here to support my brother;*
*I'm here to make my father proud;*
*I'm here to find a husband.*
*Aren't you here*
*to do the same?*

I slip
away from them, trying to swallow
my disappointment, bitter
as dandelion roots.
Is the human world
really so small
it fits inside
a corset, a jewel, a whisper?

It can't be.
I must look further;
I must learn to see
with human eyes.

The mortal world
won't tighten around me
like a fist
as the forest did,
and these girls must be greater
than they pretend to be.

**Ludwig II of Bavaria,**
the king
Richter has come so far to impress,
is obsessed with fairy tales—
boyhood stories
of doomed lovers and witches,
curses and the kisses
that break them.

Ludwig is called *the swan king*.
But if there was ever
any fierceness to him,
life has stolen it.
He sits
at the head of the ballroom,
his throne

opening around him
like the jaws of a bear.

Ludwig shrinks
from the onslaught of toasts, laughter,
jokes full of thorn-barbs.
   (As I do.)
He feels too otherworldly
for the crown
he wears here on Earth.

*I believe the king*
*would trade his title*
*to be a note in a soprano's mouth,*
*a swatch of color on a painter's canvas,*
*a single line in someone else's poem,*
Richter tells me, as his father
   (supposedly)
told him long ago.

I nod.
Ludwig, the swan king,
and I, the swan girl,
struggle to be as real, as solid, as *human*
as everyone else here.

## Chapter Twenty-Three

**I fade to the outskirts of the ballroom**
as Richter jests with boys
who all look the same.
They remind me of the steam engine,
barreling through life
without a care.

It is another group of men
who stir my interest:
the musicians
who arrange themselves beside me,
as outside the circle of conversation
          (and *belonging*)
as I am.

I lean toward them.
I know how the air feels before music
          (be it made by violins
          or the lithe footfalls of deer)
fills it.

I can't name
the human melody
these men begin to play.

But I am lost
with the first glittering note
the musicians call into being.

**The music is a rush of stardust**
flooding my mind
and the hollow stretches of my bones.
It sounds
the way a dream *feels*.

I drift
through the sparkling bevies of girls,
the golden masses of boys,
kicking off
one satin shoe
at a time.
I don't mind
the winter-chill of the floor
on my bare feet;
the summer air
I wrap around myself
warms me.

I spread my arms
as if the music could reforge my wings.
            (Though their magic is still sleeping
            in Richter's castle.)
And with laughter

sweeter than sugar or champagne
on my lips,
I dance
as I've always wanted to.

Here, I will not be
interrupted by the desperate howl
of a soul;
I will not be
torn from the music by the urgent tug
of a sister's hand.

I let myself become
a whirlwind, a burning shadow.
I roll my hips
like a river current against its bank.
I float
on the tips of my toes.

I dance until the music
dies away,
cut short like too many lives
on the forest floor.

**I open my hands and mouth**
to call the court to me,
euphoria straining against my ribs.
I want to dance

with the lords and ladies;
I want them to share in my delight!

But as I shake my damp hair
from my eyes,
blinking back the surge of red,
I realize the entire court
        is staring
                at me.

And they
are not rejoicing.

**Like the specter of a sister,**
Richter grabs my wrist and drags
        me
                out
of the ballroom and into
the hall, his boots clubbing the ground.

Nothing follows us—
except silence.

But Richter
is anything but silent himself.
Far from prying ears and eyes,
he snarls:

*What*

       *were you*

              thinking, *Hilde?*

*You told me human girls*
*can do what they want,* I snap.
*You told me human girls*
*can dance.*

*Human girls*
        *don't dance*
              *like* that.
*I thought*
*I taught you that much*
*in my castle!*
Richter grinds
his fingers into my wrist,
just hard enough
to hurt.
*Human girls don't defy gravity;*
*they don't move their bodies*
*like the sea.*
*You acted* wild,
*like you could break*
*the bones of the world*
*and reset them*
*to your liking.*

I raise my chin
like the queen Richter called me
the first time we met.
*Then how should I dance?*
*How should I be human?*
*How should I be a girl?*

Richter's voice
strains against the darkness
and his own
            scorching
temper.
*By being sweet, gentle, in control*
*of yourself.*
*If these people realize what*
*you were born as,*
*they will cast you back*
*into the forest.*
*And then you'll be a tool again,*
*alone and no different*
*than an ax, a pen, an arrow.*

My shoulders sink
like the sun under the weight
of what I understand
to be true.

I may not like
this new sharpness in Richter,
its juniper bite
aimed at me ...
but I can't deny
he's right.

I saw
the court's confusion
and the first embers of fear
in their eyes.

They know I am not
one of them.
And I need to belong
if I want to stay
in their world.

**We return to the ballroom**
and the stunned looks of the court.

I try to ignore
the chorus of whispers.
But as my gaze
moves over the crowd,
I realize
I'm being watched
with more than just unease.

A Warning About Swans

There are girls here
ready to sink their teeth
into the midnight hour,
boys so luminous
they look like beams of light.

Like me, they linger
at the fringes of the ballroom.
Unlike me, they tuck their wildness away
in the folds of their clothes,
the patchwork of their hearts.

I don't approach them;
I don't ask for their names.
But if I did, would they be:
wolf-sister, swallow-brother?
If I *did* name them, would they confess
to knowing my sisters—
tending to eggs and hatchlings with Mist,
hunting with Kara and Sigrun?

I try not to search their eyes
        (as augurs
        read the tails of comets)
for flower-strewn meadows
and the silver road in the sky.

I try not to wonder
if they are like me,
if once they could have been
my companions
as Odin's Wild Hunt was his.

## Chapter Twenty-Four

**In the long days following the dance,**
my too-quiet steps
and the softness of my voice
      (its luster
      lost somewhere
      in the halls of the Residenz)
reveal my true feelings
to Richter:
this place holds nothing I want.

His temper cool
as distant autumn,
Richter comes to me and says:
*I realize court life*
*may not suit you.*
*You aren't one*
*for rules.*

*But soon, we will leave Munich*
*and travel to other lands—*
*London, Paris, New York City.*
*Soon, we will ride*
*steam engines and ships,*
*explore all there is to see,*
*meet everyone there is to meet.*

*I only need*
*a little more time,*
*a little more gold.*
*And here, you can continue to learn*
*what it's like to be human.*
*It will make the next adventure*
*so much easier, Hilde.*

I want to believe Richter.
But the word *soon*
often sounds like a promise
made and already broken.

**I may not understand**
the girls of Munich
       (and they most certainly
       do not understand *me*)
but in their company,
I can't help but wonder:
What would my own sisters
think of life at the court?

Would Rota teach
the stiff-backed children of dukes and duchess
to swim in the Isar,
watched over by river gods
whose names have been lost
in the current?

Would Kara and Sigrun
fence with the young men,
their skirts tied
in defiant knots around their waists,
their bare and dusty feet
moving faster than their swords?

Would Eir and Mist
dance, lifted by songs
they composed as they spun
      (hand in hand)
down the mirrored hallways
lined with statues of emperors
and wonder-workers?

Would they stumble
as I have?
Would they even
have come at all?

I don't believe so.
But I have never
been like my sisters.

**I venture into the sprawling gardens**
to take my tea—
not with an exhalation of larks
or a colony of badgers,
but with human girls.

The Residenz lawn is a familiar green
but otherwise strange.

Every path is tamed;
not a branch or crocus
is out of place.
It is all order
and I feel like chaos embodied,
barely held together
by my sea-foam gown
        (masquerading
         as lace and normalcy)
and my smiles.

I ignore
the garden's unsettling perfection
and keep my secret thoughts
locked behind my new necklace—

a chain of morning dew pretending
to be a string of pearls.

These girls will be
my new kindred,
my sisters by deed
and circumstance
if not blood.
But that does not mean
I can be honest with them.

**Two of the girls, Mila and Ursula,**
arrive late to tea.
They are the same age as I am;
they wear their sixteen years
in their timid steps.

The girls each hold a painting
in their arms—
not of saints or holy maids,
but portraits of *themselves*.

*This painting of me*
*is terrible!* Mila cries.
She swoons into a chair,
attracting pitying looks
and a host of whispers.
*It looks nothing like* me!

Ursula sighs,
settling into a seat herself.
*But mine*
*is so lovely!*

*Let us see!*
*Let us see!*
The courtly ladies
        (carrion eaters
        that they are)
lean in, eager to pick apart
the paintings in question.

            Everywhere I go, I am surrounded
                by girls and birds ...
                    and those
                who are the same.

**One look at the portraits**
tells me why
Mila and Ursula are so at odds.

No one
could make the true Mila
an ugly girl—
not with a thousand mislaid brushstrokes.
But on this canvas,

her beauty
is laced with nightshade.
Painted Mila's eyes are mean,
summer-storm blue,
ready to break
over a hapless stranger's head.
Her mouth is pinched
around petty grudges and gossip.

The painting of Ursula
could not be more different.
In life,
she is the plainer of the sisters,
a girl who looks
      (perpetually)
on the brink of dissolving
into thin air.
She becomes a part of any room,
melting into
tapestries, crowds, conversations.

But in her portrait, Ursula is radiant,
her jawline cloud-soft.
The glow in her eyes
is hearth-warm,
      welcoming
love and life.

**Whoever the artist is,**
they have seen the truth
of the two sisters
and captured both girls
in body *and* spirit.

I shouldn't be so curious
about the portraits;
they are only slashes of paint
organized into girls.
But I feel more like a raven
than a swan at times.
I can't help but seek . . .
and question.

I ask the two sisters:
*Who made*
*these portraits?*

Mila and Ursula answer in unison,
and I ache for the
(lost) closeness of girls
who have grown up beneath the shadow
of the same childhood.

*Franz Mendelsohn,* the girls tell me.
*An artist*
*who's only just arrived*
*in Munich.*

Mila tosses her head
like a foal.
*Everyone who is anyone*
*is having their portrait done*
*and we had heard Mendelsohn*
*was brilliant.*
*But I doubt*
*the painter's brilliance now.*

Ursula meets my curiosity
with a hint of her own.
*I wonder*
*how Franz Mendelsohn*
*would paint you, Fräulein Hilde.*

*As red hair and strangeness.*
Mila's smirk is sharp;
it intends to draw blood from me.
           (Or, at least, tears.)
*That's all*
*Fräulein Hilde is,*
*as last week's dance made clear.*

The collective of ladies
laugh in agreement.
Like any flock, they must act
as one.

## Chapter Twenty-Five

**Richter and the boys of the court**
have been missing
all morning;
they plunged into the thin trees
surrounding the gardens
before dawn.

But as afternoon tea ends,
they pour from those near-woods,
their eyes bright
as the triggers of the rifles
they hold at the ready.

The boys approach the gardens
like an oncoming night.
But they haven't come
for *us.*

They have come
for the fox
sprinting across the lawn,
a flamelet freed from a lantern—
soon to be snuffed out
by a hound or a bullet.

I spring from my seat,
knocking over
teacups, marigold-colored macarons,
champagne flutes.
*Stop!* I call to the boys.

They don't hear me—or they won't.
They race on, overtaking
the fox

        one

        long

        stride

at a time.

I go to meet them,
my fragile skirts
hitched up around my knees,
my shoes abandoned
somewhere in the grass.

Panic burns
in the back of my throat.
What if
the fox dies here, ripped apart
in front of me
when I have no means
        (no cloak, no wings)
to help protect its body
or bring peace to its soul?

The fox must smell the woods
        (*any* woods)
on me;
it dives under the shelter
offered by my dress,
coiling around my ankles
like a chain.

The boys
        creak
                to
                        a stop.
But they don't
        lower
                their
                        rifles,
not even as I hiss:
*Stay away!*
*Leave it alone!*

(I am too much
a swan, still.)

**It is Richter who saves me**
from the boys . . .
and myself.
He stomps
to the front of the pack

(mud-stained as I am)
and slides between me
and his brothers-in-arms.

The look he gives me
could level this city;
it's a firestorm,
a gale ready to blow me away.
But Richter laughs
as he tells the boys:
*You'll have to forgive Hilde, gentlemen.*
*She has a soft spot*
*for animals.*
*We should let the fox go—*
*this time.*
*For her sake,*
*rather than the beast's.*

Foxes are born to be clever,
and this one is no different.
It knows a bargain
has been struck;
it feels it in the air
as I do.
The fox gives me a nip
(in thanks and farewell)
and bolts.

The trees swallow it
as they swallow all light that strays
too deeply into them.

**Richter refuses to speak to me**
for three days afterward.

Once, I believed silence
was a blessing.
But now it's *maddening*,
as even the wail of fading souls
never was.

I chase after Richter
as my child-self chased after Odin.
But this time, *I* am the one
offering (endless) explanations
in place of questions.

*I can be a human*
*and still care*
*about foxes, ravens,*
*the boar in the strawberry patch,* I say,
cornering Richter
behind his desk,
where he has been answering
invitations and planning
his next move—
whatever it may be.

(His court games are magpie-intricate.)

Richter's silence ends
as any deluge does:
furious, all at once.
*Be the swan*
*or be the girl, Hilde!* he barks at me.
*But you can't be both.*
*And we both know which one*
*is your cage.*

I slam
my hands on the desk;
the letters and plots tremble.
I have no use for them . . .
and they no use for me.
We are at odds,
just as Richter and I are.

*Then help me*
*to fit in as you promised,* I say.
*The ladies here*
*are having their portraits painted.*
*Hire an artist*
*to do the same for me.*
*I should remember*
*what I look like*
*as a girl.*

*It might help ground me*
*in my new life here.*

Richter drums his fingers
on the desk, as if trying to marshal
his papers to war.
*I suppose*
*it would look natural*
*for you to want a portrait.*
*I'll find an artist and then—*

*I've already found one,* I say.
*Franz Mendelsohn*
*painted many of the girls here.*
*And with great skill,*
*from what I've seen.*

## Chapter Twenty-Six

I chose the Residenz garden
as the backdrop for my portrait.

I feel more at ease
among the hyacinths and roses
than I do inside the palace.

(I hope that will change soon.)

I take my seat
on one of the marble benches,
my hands folded in my lap,
my hair spilling over my shoulders—
a fire
no dragon's hoard
of pearl clips and brooches
can contain.

I don't know how to pose.
But I'm an (unnaturally) still subject.
I must remember
to blink in the sun,
to never hold my breath for so long
I could be mistaken for
a statue or a birch.

I must remember
to be *human*.

**Franz Mendelsohn arrives**
shortly after.
The artist is younger
than I imagined—
seventeen or eighteen, like Richter.
But Franz's name isn't meant
for the history books.

The artist is knife-sharp, so thin
the wind could snap them in two.
They appear to be outgrowing the world;
their black jacket
is too small;
their pale ankles
            peek
                        out
from under
the tattered hems of their trousers.

Franz arranges their easel
in front of me.
They work quietly, striving to be
no more
than one of the flowers
in bloom around us.

Franz takes their paintbrushes
from a case
scarred by many journeys.
They handle each brush with care,
like a cygnet egg,
breakable and precious.

                        (My sister Mist,
            would appreciate this artist
                        and their gentleness.)

*I understand if you don't want to talk*
*as I paint.*
*Most of the ladies haven't.*
*But I find it awkward*
*not to at least say hello.*
Franz peers around the easel
and waves at me,
like we are both younger
and less weary.

The courtiers are stiff
as the walls they hide behind.
Seeing anyone act otherwise
makes a laugh
      (of surprise,
        of delight)
spring from my lips
before I bury it
inside me again.

      (When was the last time I laughed?
      Inside Richter's library?
      On the bank
      of Lake Forggensee?
      There has been so little joy
      here in Munich.)

*You are the only lady*
*(so far)*
*who has wanted me to paint them*
*in a garden,* Franz comments.

The artist doesn't demand
an explanation;
I give them one anyway.
*I grew up with the flowers*
*and beneath an open sky.*
*I still find comfort in both.*

Franz nods.
*I know how you feel.*
*I was born in the countryside.*
*Since then,*
*I've been to so many places—*
*so many* cities.
*But there's still something magical*
*about pine forests*
*and dusty lanes,*
*sunflower fields*
*and little rivers.*

Franz believes
we're speaking the same language;
I don't have the heart to tell them
we're not.

We never can.
Franz is the one thing
I am not—
swan or lady
cloak or no cloak:
mortal and bending
        beneath time.

**The sun climbs and Franz's brush**
        works
                in a
                        frenzy.
I imagine them painting a window
back to the fields of gold
they long for
and climbing through it.

*Do you travel often?* I ask,
if only to banish the silence
I've come to loathe.
*Do you like to follow the sunlight*
*like a cat?*

*I do.*
Franz's fingers circumnavigate
the edge of their palette,
the same way
the artist must have wandered

through country after country.
*I like the feel of a new street*
*against the bottoms of my shoes.*
*I like to see which trees*
*grow along the avenues of a city*
*I've never been to before.*
*I like houses shaped like castles*
*and wedding cakes.*
*I like to go to museums*
*and see which masterpieces*
*sailed the centuries*
*to appear on the walls.*

Franz draws in a long breath.
When they exhale,
they've transformed it into truth
after truth.
*I like seeking places*
*where I can be free.*
*Where I don't have to be*
*a boy*
*to tread new paths*
*or a girl*
*to want flowers blossoming*
*throughout my life.*

*I like discovering places*
*where I can be everything I am*

*at once,*
*where I'm not forced to fit*
*into any one shape*
*or be stained by any single color.*

*And I like arriving.*
*I like pretending*
*I'm coming home.*

**Where *is* home**
for Franz Mendelsohn?
I can hear its undertone
in the artist's voice,
and every brushstroke they make.

But I can't see its true shape.
I can only glimpse a color:
gold.

Gold as the morning,
gold as a treasure
Franz fears
they may never hold again.

*Does your family still live*
*outside the city?* Franz asks.

The truth
comes on like a fever.
*Yes, they do.*
*My five sisters*
*will always live in the woods.*
*They wouldn't dream*
*of leaving.*

*Five sisters!*
*Your life must be so full—*
*of conversation, trouble, and laughter.*
*That's what sisters give us.*
Franz twines a finger
around a lock of their hair.
*My sister was my best friend*
*and I miss her*
*the way I miss summer*
*in midwinter.*

*There are days*
*when I miss my family too,* I murmur.
*But we have to leave home*
*to find out who we are.*
*Don't we?*

Franz nods—
and we lose ourselves
in our own thoughts.
      (Of home and otherwise.)

**By the time Franz sets aside**
their paints and brushes,
my back is stiff from holding myself
sword-straight.

A rainbow smudge of paint
arches
up the side of the artist's left hand.
Another has appeared
on their cheek
where they rubbed at it earlier.
Franz is color and wonder;
they could be
someone's dream, someone's fairy tale
that only recently decided
to become real.

Franz wraps my portrait
in a tattered white cloth
and tucks it beneath their arm.
*Thank you*
*for letting me paint your portrait,*

*Fräulein Hilde.*
They bow their dark head.
*I'll send it along shortly.*

I frown.
*Can I see it*
*before you go?*

*It's . . .*
*It's not finished yet.*
Franz's cheeks
turn wildflower red.
*I want it to be*
*as close to perfect as possible*
*before I show it to you.*

We watch each other
for a moment longer.

Then Franz bows to me
a second time
and escapes—from the gardens
and the echoes of our conversation.

I wonder if
            (*when*)
I'll see them again.

## Chapter Twenty-Seven

**My portrait arrives a week later—**
without its artist.
Franz must have delivered it
and slipped away
before either Richter or I
saw them.

> (Franz is
> a most effective shadow.
> Even the foxes
> would envy
> their sly steps.)

Richter unwraps the painting,
tearing into the brown paper
as he tears through
so many other inconveniences.

But what we see beneath it
brings silence
      crashing
           down
around us.

Richter croaks:
*Did you tell Mendelsohn?*
*Did you tell the artist*
*who you really are?*

*No,* I reply,
unsure
if Richter will believe me
or not.

Because Franz Mendelsohn
has given me the very wings
I abandoned.

**The wings Franz has returned**
to my painted self
are not folded demurely.

They are spread wide,
as if I am about to free myself
from the earth and the canvas.
I do not wear the serenity
I had in the garden.
There is lightning
in my eyes and my smile.

Above me, the silver road
slashes
across a bruise-colored sky.

In the painting,
I look like the self
I'm running from:
a child of light,
more magic than love
threaded through my bones.

But how did Franz
know who
      and *what*
I am?

**I grab the canvas,**
preparing to break it
over my knee,
on the desk, under the points
of my high-heeled shoes.

But Richter grabs the painting
before I can.
*Hilde, don't.*

*Why not?*
I wanted a portrait to help me
      sink
into my new life.
But even now, I can't escape
who I was.

She is captured
in the brushstrokes,
in the mind of a stranger.

Richter takes my hand;
his touch, however gentle,
fails to lull my fear to sleep.
Its talons prick
every inch of my skin.

*To paint a beautiful girl with wings*
*may only be*
*an artist's whimsy,* Richter says.
*We'll speak*
*to this Franz Mendelsohn.*
*We'll find out their truth.*
*And we'll keep you*
            *(and our secrets)*
*safe.*

**Richter sends Franz an invitation**
to join us for tea in the garden
the next afternoon.

The gathering may take place in the open,
but it will be an interrogation,
and pity (almost) flares in me
the moment Franz sits down.

Franz's eyes
dart
from Richter's broadening grin
to the space
where my wings once were.
Are they a true threat to me
or have I let my panic
sharpen their teeth
in my mind?
The artist looks so unsure—
of themselves, their place here.

(But they know,
        they know.
                Somehow, Franz *knows*.)

**Franz ignores the tea,**
favoring sweet
after sweet.
Lemon bars, rose macarons,
and blueberries dipped in cream
all vanish
in front of Franz,
as if the artist is filling themself up
with an entire rainbow of color.

Or maybe
Franz is only trying to avoid
the conversation
they're being trapped in.

*Hilde and I*
*were impressed by the portrait.*
*What was your inspiration, Mendelsohn?*
Richter places
a hand over mine, his grin rising
like a flood.
*Why did you paint Hilde*
*with wings?*

Franz blinks
beneath their top hat.
But the velvet brim
        (old
        and moth-eaten)
doesn't offer them sanctuary.
They say softly:
*Wings seemed fitting*
*for someone so beautiful.*
*That's all.*

I keep my smile flat, calm,
Lake Forggensee embodied.
*I appreciate the compliment,*

*Franz Mendelsohn.*
*But I'm no angel.*

Richter waves a hand
at me.
Sigrun and Kara
used the same gesture to banish
the thunder from the woods.
*Yes, Hilde is only a girl,*
*like so many others*
*you've painted, Mendelsohn.*

Franz raises
their eyes,
then their voice.
*Even without wings,*
*no girl*
*is exactly*
*like any other.*
*Everyone,*
*everywhere,*
*has their own gifts.*

I tense.
But there's nothing cunning
about the wavering smile
Franz gives me.
It looks close to coming undone
under (buried) sorrow.

*Of course,* says Richter.
*I didn't mean to insult Hilde.*
*She is extraordinary . . .*
*in her own way.*

**The moment Franz leaves,**
Richter leans back
in his chair, sated by the knowledge
that our lives are unchanged—
to *him*, at least.

*There's no need*
*to worry, Hilde!*
*Franz Mendelsohn doesn't see the world*
*the way I do,* Richter says.
*The painter is mundane*
*as a stone*
*or a country road.*

But he is wrong.
Franz saw something in me—
a spark few ever have.
The artist plays the part
of being wonder-struck,
but there is more to Franz
than *this*.

Magic calls to its own;
we seek it out
in others.
But the artist's magic
makes them dangerous
to the human girl
I strive to become.

It also makes them
fascinating to the swan
who glided between worlds—
the dream-creature
I am trying
to walk away *from*.

## Chapter Twenty-Eight

**My woods excelled at keeping secrets:**
the court does not.

News of my portrait
and Franz's skills
travel forest-fire quick
through the margraves and baronesses,
the ballrooms and the gardens.

Soon, every girl and boy
wants a painting of their own,
wings to wear, a hint of the ethereal
in their smiles.

But after me,
Franz chooses
only the most conventional subjects—
the girls who dream
of a kiss and a wedding dress,
the boys who laugh
like gunfire
and wear their bruises as medals.

The artist avoids
the sharper girls, the boys gentle as sighs,
the ones who may
       (or may not)
be as eternal as I am.

Franz makes no excuses
for turning away the most unusual of us.
They simply offer apologies—
       *I'm sorry,*
       *I'm sorry,*
       *I'm sorry.*

Richter grumbles
over Franz's lack of ambition,
as if it might be catching.
*That idiot could be rich!* he mutters.
*It doesn't make sense*
*why Mendelsohn will paint some courtiers*
*and not others.*

But I think
I understand Franz.
If they see the truth of everyone
when they have a paintbrush
in hand,
they're wise to be wary
of what they might learn.

They've already learned
so much
          (too much)
about *me.*

## Chapter Twenty-Nine

**I never intended to seek out**
King Ludwig for myself;
I never wanted to see
my portrait again.

But I find both waiting for me
in the gilded rooms
       (all silk wallpaper and soft sheets)
Richter and I share.

I should feel awed
in the presence of a king
(supposedly) chosen
by something greater
than sea or sky
to rule Bavaria.

I'm not.
Ludwig is gossamer and glitter,
stretched too thin across his kingdom
and country.
He is fragile . . .
and desperate not to be.

**King Ludwig turns to me,**
his smile a ghost
of what it should be.

*I was just admiring your portrait.*
*You are Fräulein Hilde, yes?*
*Baron von Richter's companion?*
*I knew his father well.*
*We were close,*

*once upon a time,*
*as you and his son are close now.*

Was Ludwig drawn
to Richter's father
the same way I was drawn
to his son?
Did the first baron
promise the king happiness
and pour gold into his hands
in its place?

I hide
these questions
       (too personal, too dangerous)
under my tongue.
*I came here*
*with Baron von Richter, yes.*

Ludwig nods
but he does not take his eyes
off my portrait.
*This is beautiful work;*
*it has captured the true feel of you.*
*You remind me*
*a little of myself, Fräulein Hilde.*
*I would have preferred*
*to stay in the woods*

*where I was born.*
*Is the same true of you?*

My voice mimics
a swallow's carefree song
as I give my answer:
*No, Your Royal Highness.*
*I'm perfectly happy*
*right where I am.*

It's not
　　　　　(exactly)
a lie.
But it's not
　　　　　(exactly)
the truth either.

## Chapter Thirty

**It comes as no great surprise**
that the next person to summon Franz
is King Ludwig himself.

The courtiers chatter like sparrows
as Franz shuffles through
the golden audience chamber.

The artist looks (too) vulnerable
without their paints and canvas
to hide behind.

*Thank you for inviting me,*
*Your Royal Highness.*
Franz's hair
tumbles over their brow
as they bow to the king,
their eyes hare-wide with fear.

But Franz
shouldn't be afraid.
Ludwig is neither hunter nor hound,
and his regal nod
comes no more naturally to him
than waltzing comes to me.

Ludwig says:
*I have a request, Franz Mendelsohn.*
*I'm building a new palace,*
*Neuschwanstein,*
*near the village of Füssen.*
*It will be a tribute*
*to Bavaria's greatest stories.*
The king strains forward
on his throne.
*But the castle needs an artist*

*to capture those stories*
*on its many walls.*
*Will you paint for me?*
*Will you use your gift*
*and make my palace*
*a true fairy tale?*

Franz's face
turns milk-and-heaven white.
*I . . .*
*I'm honored,*
*Your Royal Highness.*
*But I'm young,*
*only an amateur.*
*Your palace deserves*
*a better artist than* me.

*But it's you I want,* says Ludwig.
*It's you*
*who should paint it!*
*You understand magic*
*in a way others*
*do not.*

I bite back a laugh.
Of course Franz does.
They are
        (they *must* be)
a little magical themself.

**Richter nods at Franz,**
his brow
weighed down by the jewels
I crafted for him.
*If you agree to paint*
*for His Royal Highness,*
          *(as I'm sure you will)*
*you can stay with me*
*and Hilde at my castle,* Richter says.
*It's not far*
*from Füssen.*

The entire court
          (myself included)
pivots to stare at Richter.
His voice is the last one
I expected to hear
ringing out.

I want to grab Richter
with talons I no longer have.
Does he not understand the threat
Franz could pose to us both,
how difficult it is for me to be
in the company of magic
and stay even close to human?

Ludwig speaks
before I can, his voice softer
than any phantom's.
*That's very generous,*
*Baron von Richter.*

*I'm always happy to help*
*my king,* Richter says,
flashing a smile.

The king stares at Richter
for too many breaths.
Does he see
a hint of the first baron
in the boy's stance?

I believe he must;
I recognize the feel of a haunting
better than most.

Franz Mendelsohn clears their throat.
*Thank you, Baron von Richter.*
*You're most kind.*
*And, Your Royal Highness . . .*
*I'll give you*
*my answer soon.*

## Chapter Thirty-One

The courtiers, vultures that they are,
disperse the moment there are no more
conversations, arguments, rumors
to be ripped apart and examined.

As for Franz, the artist vanishes
before anyone can corner them.
Only I see where Franz goes;
only I follow them.

> (Maybe it's safer
> to keep your secrets close.
> And Franz is the keeper
> of all mine.)

In their dark coat and suit,
          ill-fitting and threadbare,
Franz should look dreary
in the Marienplatz,
adrift in the sea of roses.

Somehow, they *don't*.
Franz is the stroke of midnight,
faintly touched by stars,
and I watch them from the street corner
with (too much) interest.

All creatures are curious
about the nature of our undoing.
A mouse can't help but admire
the shining eyes of a snake;
even a doe can appreciate
a strain of wolf-song.

And I
        (neither this nor that)
am no exception.

**I glide past vendors and puppeteers,**
peasants and café poets,
and up to Franz.

A question leaves my lips
before I can swallow it.
*Will you accept*
*the king's patronage?*
*Will you paint stories*
*at his castle?*

Franz removes their hat,
revealing
the landscape of their face,
winter-lean and pale.
Their gaze
shimmers,

pierced by the same enchanted light
found in my own,
in Ludwig's,
in the girls with jagged edges
and those of the spring-soft boys
at court.


*I want to, Fräulein Hilde.*
*But I'm afraid,* Franz confesses.
*What if my imagination*
        *(and my skills)*
*fall short?*
*And well . . .*
*I'm a Jew.*
*In the fairy tales*
*King Ludwig has built his castle*
*and his kingdom on,*
*to be a Jew is to be*
        *a thief, a swindler, a witch,*
        *waltzing myself bloody*
        *in someone else's thorns.*
*In the king's stories,*
*I'm doomed to be*
*the monster.*


I am too, in a way.
Feral girls
        (roots in their veins,

        leaves in their hair)
are unfit to be heroines.

*Then make the fairy tales*
*your own,* I say to Franz—
and yes, to myself.
*Take them back.*
*Transform yourself*
*into their hero.*
*And if you paint for the king,*
*your eyes and imagination*
*won't fail you.*
*You see*
*too clearly for that.*

*And you'll be there,* whispers Franz.
*With Baron von Richter,*
*at his castle.*

**I'm toying with a knife,**
I'm dancing with a lightning strike,
I'm playing with an end
to my time as a girl.

Franz is the only person
who can expose my secret
and crush
my (nearly) human life

before it has a chance to flower.
Yet by now,
the artist could have whispered
the truth
      (of me)
into the ears of a dozen courtiers.
And
      they
           haven't.

In my hidden heart
of hearts,
I don't believe they *will*.

*Yes, Franz,* I confirm.
*I'll be at Richter's castle.*

Franz dons
their hat again.
*Then I'll paint*
*King Ludwig's stories.*

They take their leave of me
and the square,
accompanied by the bells
of the cathedral
tolling out the hour.
This time, I do not follow.
But I am (ever) watchful.

Hold my secret close, Franz Mendelsohn.

And I

will do the same.

THE THIRD TALE

THE CASTLE ON THE HILL

### Chapter Thirty-Two

**The carriage ride from Munich,**
my first carriage ride ever,
is unsettling.

Sickness grows,
green moss in my belly,
whenever we turn a sharp corner,
and the smell of the horse
overwhelms me as an animal's scent
never has before.

Before Munich, Richter,
portraits, and jewels,
my sisters and I slept in lynx dens,
pine martens draped over our shoulders,
their musk our perfume.

But the horse
smells of iron, fear, the leather whip
driving it onward;
I can't help pitying it.

Richter and I sit side by side,
our hips
digging into one another's.
The boy's eyes have glazed over
with boredom.
He doesn't notice
my discomfort ... or anyone else's.

Franz studies
their paint-dabbled hands
          (as if the echoes
          of reds and blues
          will give up
          the secrets of the world)
while King Ludwig's mist-colored eyes
shift between the three of us
in turn.

Three is a number of power.
But what kind of power
will our strange trio
          (boy, artist, swan—
          the stuff of unfinished tales)
conjure for this king?

**Ludwig takes our new triumvirate**
to tour the palace he is building.
True to his word,
it's not far from Lake Forggensee
and Richter's shambling home.

I didn't think any building
crafted by mortal hands
could surpass Munich's hundred spires.
But Neuschwanstein Castle is dream-dazzling,
standing in defiance
of the harsher world around it.

Its white walls
surge like waves
against the rugged hillside;
its towers could hold
a sleeping princess, a dragon,
the endless histories of both.

The architects and carpenters
striding back and forth
across the palace grounds
are magicians in their own right.
They unravel
      trees,
      stones,

slabs of marble,
and carve a story from each.

I move from worker to worker,
marveling
at what they have done.
They are all creators, their power
vast as the sky.
           (As mine is not.)
Each is no less talented
than Odin himself.

*Every room in Neuschwanstein*
*will be dedicated*
*to a fairy tale,* Ludwig explains
as we walk through
the palace's many tangled halls.
*Perhaps the knight Siegfried*
*will battle dragons*
*on the walls of the dining hall.*
*Flights of angels*
*might trail stars behind them*
*in my throne room.*
*The lower hall*
*could tell the story of a man*
*who learned the language of birds*
*in silver and gold paint.*

Franz and I are easily lost
in the king's wonder tales.
But the moment Ludwig
       (that will-o'-the-wisp
       trapped
       in the body of a man)
leaves us,
Richter's lip curls
like a dying rose petal.
*The king is a fool;*
*this castle is a waste*
*of time*
*and money!*

*Maybe you're right,* I say.
*But it's also beautiful.*
*What is time*
*if not yours to waste?*
*What is money*
*if not yours to spend?*

I don't miss
Franz's wordless agreement:
a small, lilting smile.
(But I pretend to.)

## Chapter Thirty-Three

**Richter's own castle**
remains stubbornly unlovely
and unchanged.

It doesn't celebrate our arrival,
but that is only fair;
I'm too exhausted to greet it
and show its tired magic
the respect it (perhaps) deserves.

*We won't stay here long,* Richter assures me.
      (And, I suspect, himself.)
*Just long enough*
*for the artist to finish the murals.*
*Then we'll go*
*wherever you want.*

But I don't touch
the army of trunks and suitcases
we've carried
from Munich, each one bursting
with rose-petal dresses
and crystalline stars to string
in my hair.

*I could leave now,* I suggest.
*Your wealth is greater*
*than even the king's*
*and I believe*
*I've learned*
*what it means to be human.*

*Please, don't go yet!*
The words burst
            (unexpected)
from Richter's lips
like flowers from the earth.
*The dappled light of some*
*other*
            *world*
*still bleeds through you—*
*which means I*
*can still help you.*
*And I . . .*
The boy's gaze darts aside, mouse-swift
and just as desperate
not to be *seen* for what it is.
*I would miss you*
*if you were gone.*

We study one another,
the moment stretching on
until I snap it with a mouthful

of words—and teeth.
*I'm in no hurry*
*to be alone again.*
*But I won't wait here*
*forever.*
*I want more freedom*
*than your castle can give.*

Richter opens one of my trunks,
his smile reigniting.
*As*

        *do*

*I.*

**That night, I toss, I turn, I doze,**
restless
as one of my feathers
caught in a gale.

I should welcome
the purple oblivion of sleep;
I might find peace in its depths.
But my thoughts
roar and rage
too loudly for me to calm . . .
and my cloak
beckons from the wardrobe.

I climb
out of bed and open the doors.
Time hasn't dimmed
my cape's starlit threads.
It awakens, whispering
as I pull it against my chest:
*Do not deny*
*your true self, your wildness, your strength.*
*Do not deny*
*the love you have*
*for the boar in the strawberry patch,*
*the foxes hunted by the hounds.*
*Take to the sky,*
*take your sisters in your arms again.*
*Discard that boy*
*and his promises and return*
*to the woods.*

I hiss
and bury the cloak
in the darkest corner of the wardrobe.

*I'm more*
*than the lonely ending*
*to another creature's days,* I mutter.
*I'm more*
*than my father's daughter.*
*I'm more*

*than one sister*
*ignored by all the others.*
*Now let me be.*

**Distractions are easy to come by**
in this strange castle.
Franz is only the latest.

The artist is standing in the long corridor
outside my room,
framed by the rising sun.

Franz holds
four fringes of the white shawl
draped around their shoulders,
swaying in time with the breeze.
A chant
unfurls from their lips
in a language
unknown in the forest.

The shawl transforms the artist
as my own cloak
changes me;
it makes their edges glow.

I want to tell Franz
I, too, used to ride the wind

and ask them how they learned
the trick of it themself.

> (I want to stitch my lips closed
> around the artist
> and the subject of magic
> for all time.)

**Sensing me, Franz's chant stops**
abruptly.
They drop the fringes of their cloak
and peek up at me
through charcoal-dark lashes.
*Did I wake you?*
*I'm sorry, Fräulein Hilde.*
*I was praying.*

It's not lost on me how Franz
prays to the east, to the future,
while I seem to face the west,
the woods and the past,
without fail.
*I don't pray myself,* I tell them.

> (Who would I pray to?
> Which gods
> will answer strange girls
> when their own fathers won't?)

*But I envy*
*that you believe in anything enough*
*to thank it*
*for the new day.*

Franz gulps down a breath,
like I've brought the lake with me
and they are drowning
in the incoming tide.
*Would you like to come with me*
*to Neuschwanstein,*
*Fräulein Hilde?* they manage to ask.
*You seemed to enjoy being there*
*yesterday.*

I

   descend

     into silence
and the secrets
lying in wait for me there.
But inside Ludwig's palace,
my cloak can't tempt me
with its quiet magic
and I'll be tethered
to this world, not the one
I shed.

It is safer to go
than to stay here.
*Thank you, Franz.*
*I would like that*
*very much.*

## Chapter Thirty-Four

**The first room**
King Ludwig has instructed
Franz to paint
is his bedchamber.

Its lean oak panels are twined together,
reminding me of my woods
in miniature.
A golden chandelier
hangs from the ceiling,
a second sun no less brilliant
than a true star.
A silver-plated swan
hovers over the washstand,
comforting me with the familiar,
mocking me with her wings.

But any discomfort I feel
is nothing compared to Franz's.
They stare
at the room's blank walls
as others would gaze at a monster.
Beauty
            (and the possibility of it)
can inspire
both terror and reverence.

The artist swallows.
*I've never had a canvas*
*this large before.*
*There's so much space*
*I can use to create.*
*I don't even know*
*where to begin!*

*You can begin*
*as many times as you like,* I say.
*That's the best part*
*about beginnings—*
*they're infinite.*

            (But there can be
            only a single ending.)

Franz laughs—or tries to;
the sound rattles in their throat.
*You're right.*
*And this castle*
*is truly the perfect place*
*to begin.*
*It's so quiet on this hillside,*
*so still.*
*Even the trees*
*are holding their breath.*

I try not to look
at the washstand's silver swan.
*They might be.*
*The trees in any wood*
*know more*
*than they like to let on.*

**Franz dips their brush**
in the blue paint they've mixed,
only to pause, the tip
       poised
above the wall.
*Take my hand, Hilde.*
*Please?*
*I want us*
*to do this together.*
*It was you*

*who brought me here!*
*It was you*
*who gave me*
*this new future.*

I don't want to take credit
for Franz's work
or even their luck.
I don't want to entwine myself
in someone who sees too much
of who I was.

But there is a hollowness
lurking
behind the artist's eyes,
and Franz is too kind
to be filled with these shadows
          (gray as smoke
            and mourning cries)
alone.

I fold my hand
over Franz's
and our (twin) hearts
          quicken
in unison.
I pretend not to hear
Franz's gasp.

I pretend
I didn't want to do the same
the instant
I touched the artist.

Stilling our hearts
as one
            (stilling my doubts)
Franz and I paint the first blue line
on the horizon.

**I didn't believe a boy could ever be**
a weapon.
But when I walk through
the castle gates
as morning bleeds into afternoon,
Richter
            (lean and unbending,
            his grace sharp)
feels no different
than the bow and arrow
he is toying with
in the courtyard.

*Where were you?* Richter barks.
Each word is a barb
he aims at a single target: me.
*Do you crave magic*

*so much that you wandered*
*back into the woods?*

> (Jealousy is a thorn;
> it pricks
> the heart of its owner—
> and those around them.
> But I was not expecting
> to be cut by Richter's.)

*I only left*
*to watch Franz paint*
*at Neuschwanstein,* I protest.
*It helps me*
*keep my feet on the ground,*
*my past still*
*at the back of my throat.*
*It keeps me away from the sky.*
*It keeps me* human.

Richter tosses his bow
> (and his bruising looks)
aside, his shoulders
slumping.
His anger leaves him quickly,
as all poison must,
lest it kill.
*I'm sorry, Hilde.*

*I don't want to lose you*
*to the woods or anything else.*

Now that his hands are empty,
Richter reaches for mine
to fill them.
*I need you, Hilde.*
*I've always needed you, long before*
*we ever met.*
*You were my first*
*true friend.*

I run my fingers through Richter's . . .
but I don't let them

                        linger.

He has become
so desperate for me
since we returned—
but does he need *me*?

Or could his cravings
         (left unsatisfied by treasure)
be sated by any girl,
any glimmer of wonder?

It is becoming
difficult to tell.

## Chapter Thirty-Five

**In the days that follow,**
I see Franz's mural take shape,
one line, one figure, one leaf
at a time.

The artist's subjects
are from a legend:
that of Lady Isolde
and the knight Tristan.

Franz told me about these doomed lovers
as we traveled up
the hillside path
leading to Neuschwanstein.

*Tristan and Isolde*
*loved one another*
*with the fierceness of summer,*
*the endlessness of the sea.*
*But Lady Isolde*
*was engaged to a king,*
*and Tristan*
*was no more than a knight*
*serving that same ruler.*

*After many trials,*
*Tristan died,*
*poisoned by his enemies.*
*And Isolde's heart*
            *(and life)*

                        *broke*

*at the exact moment*
*her beloved met his end.*


            (The human world
        is no different from the woods.
                It is full
        to bursting with its own tragedies—
                both real
            and imagined.)


**In Franz's mural of Tristan and Isolde,**
the lovers are entwined
in each other's arms,
about to be fulfilled by a kiss ...
or undone by it.

I scowl at them;
I see nothing here
but the beginning of
yet another ending.

*King Ludwig gave you a choice*
*about which story to paint.*
*What drew your imagination*
*to this story, Franz?*

Franz's paintbrush
moves like a cat's tail,
restless and precise.
They don't dare look away
from their work,
a sunlit window into a place of love
and deeper loss.

> (Franz may fear
> the story will escape them
> if they do.)

*I like romances.*
*Don't you, Hilde?*

I shrug,
a most
unladylike act.

> (But with Franz, I'm no lady
> pretending at mortality.
> I'm only *Hilde*, only myself—
> whoever, whatever that may be.)

*I don't trust them.*
*Especially not romances*
*like Tristan and Isolde's.*

*They gained nothing from their love*
*but the breaking*
*of their hopes, bones, lives.*

Franz knocks
their bare heels together.
The bottoms of their feet
are dusky pink.
They must have wandered
across their own pallet earlier.
      (In search of *what*?)
*I could give Tristan and Isolde*
*a happy ending,*
*one where they walk out of their tale*
*and into the morning light,*
*hand in hand.*

*But would it be a lie?*
      (And can Franz
      even paint something
      untrue?)

The artist shakes their head.
*I don't think so.*
*Maybe* this *Isolde*
*and* this *Tristan*
*are destined*
*for a different life.*

*A* better *life.*
*I'd like to believe it's so.*

**As they work, Franz teaches me**
the secret names of the colors
they make marvels with.
Blue alone
comes in a dozen shades.
        *Berlin* and
*paradise,*
                *eggshell* and
*sea glass.*

Red, too, has many hues.
*Your hair is* ember, *Hilde.*
Franz traces the shape of it
in the air,
only to lower their hand.

We haven't touched
since the first day
we painted together.
I won't allow myself
to cross that line again.
I am not Franz's future—
and they are not mine.

*And* your *hair?* I ask,
desperate to escape my own
       (spiraling, swan-diving)
thoughts.
*What color is it?*

Franz loops a dark strand
around their finger.
*Black as the words*
*printed in a book,*
*black as the nights*
*when a tale's needed the most.*
*You see, me and my People*
*are made of more stories*
*than dust.*

       (I can relate, little
       as I like to.)

**I sprawl out**
on the floor of the king's bedchamber.
My ankles show;
my hair is all snarls.
I've come as I am,
as I've tried not to be ...
       (and failed
       in so many ways).

But unlike Richter and the court,
Franz has never demanded
anything else from me.

*Of all the places*
*you've gone,* I say,
*what was your favorite, Franz?*

Franz spreads their hands,
a curtain opening
on a scene from their history.
*The best city is Berlin.*
*Like the name of the color.*
*There's a park in it, grand*
*as a forest,*
*filled with statues of lions*
*and golden angels.*
*I climbed them, half believing*
*I could fly away*
*on their wings.*

*Maybe the statues*
*came to life*
*after you left,*
*inspired by your belief,* I say.

But Franz is quick
to protest.
*I'm no magician.*

I stretch,
my bare toes
pointed like a ballerina's—
or a falcon's.
*All artists are.*
*If there's anything*
*being here has taught me,*
*it's that.*
*You should believe*
*in yourself, Franz.*
*I do.*

I look away, pretending
not to see Franz
rubbing at their pink cheeks,
trying to will
the color away.

But is there anything louder than silence
between friends?

## Chapter Thirty-Six

**Franz begins leaving drawings**
in places they know only I
will think to look.

I discover the sketches
tucked in my shoes,
the hoods of my cloaks,
the hollow of the tree
standing at attention
beneath my bedroom window.

Franz speaks to me in charcoal lines
and dabs of color,
portraits dipped
in purple and gold.

They draw Ludwig,
a swan in his Munich garden,
his golden crown replaced
by a circlet of white roses.

They draw Neuschwanstein
as a lion, sinking
its white claws into the hillside.

But Franz's most common subject
is Richter.

He draws Richter
as a whirlpool, his belly bottomless—
regardless of how many mermaids
he drags into it.

R. M. Romero

He draws Richter
as a snake, forever eating
its own tail,
his eyes containing less
than a fistful of ash,
his hands trying to hold
more than the sky.

Franz draws Richter
as the warning
they won't say aloud.

I've had my fill of warnings;
my sisters and Odin
gave them all too freely.

But I keep each of Franz's sketches,
hiding them
in the back of my wardrobe
beside my cloak, another secret
that burns when I hold it
against my heart.

**Richter lays out maps and plots**
in the castle library, once a sanctuary—
*our* sanctuary.
Now, it is a theater
for him to perform in.

His footfalls
are heavy as he paces;
he has learned to take up the space
he believes
he was born to stand in.

But I
            (his most captive audience)
feel smaller than ever.

I sought
freedom with Richter.
But the only time I feel free now
is when I'm with Franz,
my body and words untamed.

Richter says:
*I want*
*the ambassadorship to the Hapsburg Court.*
*I want*
*to open new businesses in Budapest.*
*I want*
*the king's ear above all others.*
*I want, I want, I want*
*to see how much of the world*
*we can have.*

**I interrupt Richter's litany of desires,**
asking him:
*Where is the boy whose lips*
*were scarred with stories?*
*Where is the boy*
*who promised me my freedom?*
*I don't see him*
*here with me.*
*(Anymore.)*

I sigh, my shoulders sinking
beneath my weariness.
*I think it's time*
*we parted ways, Richter.*
*I don't want to own*
*any corner of this world.*
*I only*
*want to own* myself.

Richter's pacing
            ceases.
He stumbles
to me, looking
            (too much)
like Franz's drawings,
empty and half starved.
*Hilde, please!*
*You wanted a life*

*bigger than one contained*
*in moldering bones*
*and groves of pine trees.*
*I said*
*I would give you that life,*
*change you from mere lore*
*to a lady.*
*Haven't I*
*kept my promise?*

*Maybe.*
*But the life*
*you're fighting for now*
*isn't the life I want, I say.*

The words
bring Richter
to his knees before me,
his face crumbling
like the empires once ruled
            (since lost)
by his ancestors.
*I can do better by you, for you.*
*Hilde, you and I*
*were destined to meet;*
*you and I*
*were destined to stay together.*
*Don't leave (me) now!*
*I can't be alone (again)!*

**It would be so much easier**
if it *were* destiny
binding me to Richter,
a thread
forged from the strength of
        magic, love,
        the place
        where the two meet.

But it isn't.

I say
        (more softly
        than he deserves):
*We met by chance, Richter.*
*And I'm tired of being*
*just another jewel*
*for you to display.*
*I don't belong*
*to you, Richter.*

The boy
        (no man, no one so strong)
balls his hands around
my gown of mist, rending it.
*It's not like that!*

*Please*

                    *don't*

           *leave*

*me!*

*I've given you everything*

*I have to give, Hilde!*

*Beautiful things, a new home,*

*the chance to be adored.*

*I did everything*

*I was supposed to do*

*to make you*

*STAY!*


I stand, looking down

at Richter,

at the tears (false or true?)

gathering on his lashes.

I should be moved by them.


       (I am not.)


I let

Richter's hands and pleas

       fall away.

*I need time*

*to think,* I tell him.

*About* my *wants,* my *needs,* my *desires.*

*But if I choose to leave,*

*I will say goodbye*
*before I do.*

## Chapter Thirty-Seven

**My argument with Richter**
is still an unhealed wound
when the boys from the court
      (charmed
         by his riches and golden smiles)
come to visit him.

These fellow barons and margraves
wear their furs and ambitions
openly.
Why shouldn't they?
They are all that the(ir) world embraces—
young and handsome, proud
as stags.

But Richter doesn't allow
the other boys
near his family's castle.
It is too close to his heart
and too much *like* it—

weathered
but unbroken,
breeding haggard shadows.

Instead, Richter meets the boys
for a picnic and a hunt
near Lake Forggensee.
The dukes will not judge the waters
for their lack of ornate trim.
The counts will not cringe back
from the darkness
spread by the yew trees.

No one will see
anything
but what Richter wants them to.

**I won't participate in the hunt.**
Even if I wanted to,
it would be unseemly for the lady
the boys assume I am
(one whose hands
have never been soaked in blood)
to take up a rifle.

But I want to wade
in the lake
and listen to the waves speak

as I used to.
Water holds both memory and wisdom:
it may give me
the clarity I long for.


So with the pine needles
crackling beneath my heels,
the riotous laughter of the other boys
choking me
like smoke,
I walk down to the lake
beside Richter.


*I know*
*we're having difficulties,*
murmurs Richter.
*But I appreciate you being here.*
*(With me.)*
*And to show you my appreciation—*
he catches me,
by surprise, by the wrist—
*I promise*
*to come back from the hunt*
*empty-handed.*


I wish
Richter would make his vow
in the forest way,

with a prick of tooth and claw.
But he's no son of the woods.

Still, I want to trust this boy
         (one last time)
not to harvest
something else's death.
He *did* spare the fox
in Munich;
he has no reason
not to be merciful again.

I nod at Richter.
*Thank you.*
I do *appreciate it.*

**The lakeside isn't empty.**
Franz is sitting on the bank,
         folded
around their sketchbook
as if they, too, have wings.

A crown of white flowers
rests on their head.
Did Franz braid it for themself
or did a nearby meadow
decide they could rule it

for a day,

an hour,

an instant?

*Shouldn't you be working?*
Richter's frown
is deep as the lake.
*The king isn't paying you*
*to daydream, Mendelsohn.*

Franz holds up their sketchbook.
The look in their eyes is the same one
that must have ignited
in Tristan's
when he leaned in
to kiss Isolde
for the very first time.

It is a look
called *courage.*

*I* am *working,* says Franz.
*I need to study the trees here*
*so I can paint them*
*at Neuschwanstein.*
*And that*
*is exactly*
*what the king is paying me for.*

I bite back
a smirk.
I like the velvet softness
of Franz Mendelsohn . . .
but I like this (new) spark
of defiance, too.

**One of the courtly boys**
strides up to Franz
and jabs them with his elbow.
*You look so serious!*
*Perhaps you should daydream*
*a little more.*
*Come hunt with us,*
*since you're here.*

Franz's shoulders
curl around their pale cheeks.
If they could melt
away like snow,
I think they would.
*I'm sorry.*
*I have work to do.*
*But thank you*
*for the invitation.*

The boys from court shrug,
a collective

of confusion.
They've never had to work
for anything.
It shows
in the unbroken skin of their palms,
in their pale faces. their white-gold locks.
These are boys
who only drink in the sun
when they want to.
They have never walked or labored
beneath it
out of necessity.

I look back
at Richter and Franz—
their rough hands,
the freckles marking their cheeks
like strings of constellations.

Hardship made these two
different; loneliness filled them
long before
words of love.

But I believe
it only made one of them
kind.

**Richter departs with his pack of boys,**
all yipping like hounds.

The wind tugs
at Franz's sketchbook.
The corners of the pages
curl eastward, trying to coax the artist
back up the hill to Neuschwanstein.
They don't follow it;
they turn (instead) to me.
*Would you like me to stay*
*with you, Hilde?*

Is this a misguided attempt
at knightly virtue,
an opportunity for Franz to pretend
they are Tristan?
Do they think
I (of all creatures)
need to be protected
from the yew trees and the lake?

One glance at Franz
tells me the truth:
they don't want me to be
left behind, solitude stranded
beside these waters.

*You can stay, Franz.*
*It would be nice*
*to have some company.*

## Chapter Thirty-Eight

**The sun has barely moved**
when Richter and the others
stomp back to the lake.

Sweat is beaded along Richter's temples,
a mirror of the diamonds
he's so proud to wear.
He drags
his bow behind him, unsettling
the earth.

But what unsettles *me*
is the corpse of a deer,
thrown carelessly
over Richter's shoulder.

The boy puffs out his chest,
a pheasant preening for his mate.
*The deer put up*
*quite a fight!* he says

to me,
the boys,
the body in his arms.
*But I*
*was stronger*
*in the end.*

I've seen
a hundred corpses before,
a chorus of flies
buzzing over their heads.
But never
like this,
never accompanied
by a smile.

Wolves don't boast
over their kills;
ravens don't invent epics
about how they came by their suppers.
Their hunger
is simple.

*My* hunger
was simple.
But Richter's is not.

A snarl climbs into my mouth,
ready to pounce
on Richter.
But it's Franz who clamps a hand
against their lips.

I feel
the burn of sickness
in the artist's throat,
the warmth of their tears
as if we share our bones
in addition
to (some of) our secrets.

Franz scrambles
off the ground, their sketchbook
                        falling
onto the muddy bank.
The artist
is no kin to the deer—
not as I am.
But maybe its spirit
has snuck under Franz's skin,
allowing them to leap
free of the hunters
and delve into the yew trees.

Richter's composure splinters
in a different way.

He bursts out laughing,
the sound no different
than gunfire;
it's made to injure.
The boys from court
accompany him, not wanting to be laughed at
themselves.

*It was only*
*an animal,* sneers Richter.
*Why does Mendelsohn care*
*so much?*

*And what do you think* I *am,*
*if not an animal?*
I growl, too quietly
for the dukes and lords to hear.
                (I am, after all,
                kin to wolves.)

My words hit their mark
and Richter
cringes.
*You're different,* he tries.
*I never meant ...*

But it's the wrong thing to say.
I spit
at his feet, no more (false) lady
left in me.
*I'm* no *different.*
*But you* are, *Richter.*
*Today has proven* that.

Without my cloak here,
I can't fly into the yews
eager to welcome me.
But I can toss my head,
hair blazing
as if struck by a match
and march

      away

         from Richter.

## Chapter Thirty-Nine

**I'm afraid I'll find Franz**
crouched in the strawberry patch
where I left the bones of the boar.

     (And my old life.)

But Franz hasn't strayed
too deeply
into the little copses of trees.
They have taken shelter
under the pale arms of a birch,
their head
        (the flowers
           absent from its crown)
cradled
in (forever) paint-smudged hands.

*Did I embarrass you, Hilde?*
Franz speaks
from between their fingers
and around their sorrow.
*I'm sorry if I did.*
*I was just so upset!*
*That poor deer.*

I duck
beneath the birch,
wishing
it could enfold Franz and me,
a shield against the world.
*Don't apologize.*
*I wanted to cry too.*
*That deer wasn't killed*
*for meat or warmth.*

*It shouldn't have had to die*
*because Richter wanted to prove*
*how strong he was.*

*But you didn't cry.*
Franz lifts
their eyes, their tears bright
as raindrops.
Has their life
been a series of thunderstorms
         (barely weathered)
until now?
I wonder.

*I've always turned my tears*
*into screams,*
*made anger*
*out of my sadness,* I reply.
*But sometimes, crying*
*and showing*
*the moss-soft parts of yourself*
*is much braver*
*than trying to be stone.*

**Franz drags their knees**
up against their chest, making themself
whisper-small.
*Boys have always called me*

*too soft;*
*most girls*
*just laughed at me.*
*Before you,*
*there was only one person*
*who didn't:*
*my sister, Golda.*

*She told me once*
*we're each born with a miracle,*
*something about us that glitters*
*and can never be rotted away*
*by bitterness.*
*Golda's miracle was her music;*
*mine might be my art.*

Franz's gaze
is clouded with history,
their lashes long as roads
I haven't traveled.
        (Will I ever?)

The artist murmurs
to me, to themselves,
to the birch:
*I wonder how many times*
Golda's *soul*
        circled

*the world*
*for her*
*to have become so wise.*

**The tale Franz gives me**
is like one of his sketches—
incomplete, lacking a true ending.

> (I can still sense
> true endings
> as others sense storms
> riding over the mountains.)

*Golda and I were raised*
*by our uncle.*
*He wasn't a bad man.*
*He gave to charity;*
*he took me and Golda in*
*with a smile after we lost*
*our parents.*

*We never wanted*
*for apples and honey,*
*for winter clothing,*
*for sheets of music*
*or paint.*

*But our uncle*
*was a furrier*
*and I cried*
*the first time he brought*
*new pelts*
> *(stoat and fox,*
>> *wolf and rabbit)*
*to his shop.*

*I tried to coax the animals*
*back to life.*
*I thought I could will*
>> *a spark*
*back*
*into their eyes*
*if I wished hard enough.*

*But the furs*
*remained furs, no soul*
*tucked inside them.*
*So I ran*
*from my uncle's shop,*
*down the road*
*to the little house*
*where we lived*
*and the animals never would.*

*Golda was at her piano,*
*her fingers dancing on the keys,*
*fast as ravens.*

*I watched my sister play,*
*watched her glow.*
*Her hair*
*was the color of amber,*
*red and gold,*
*her smile radiant.*

*When Golda saw my tears,*
*she played a string of notes*
*again and again,*
*louder and louder.*
*And I*
*let myself*
*be lifted up by them.*

**Franz interrupts**
their own story with a whistle.

The short burst of song
makes my bones
thrum.
It sounds like Eir's melodies,
shining
and triumphant.
*What was that?*

*Notes in the major seventh chords*
*and the key of F.*
Franz's smile returns.
*Golda said those notes*
*are the happiest sounds*
*in the entire world.*
*They're how*
*she stopped my tears*
*on the day the first furs came.*

*But afterward,*
*I still thought about the animals.*
*I even dreamed*
*I was one of them:*
*a fox*
*with fur the color of marigolds*
*outrunning the hunters,*
*racing the night.*

*What happened*
*to your sister?* I ask.

Franz swallows,
saying nothing.
And that
            in turn
says *everything.*

I try a different question,
one whose answer
won't send cracks
through Franz's troubled heart.
*Can you sing*
*your sister's notes again?*
*I want to learn them myself.*

Light seeping in
to their wavering smile,
Franz does.

**The notes still hanging in the air,**
the artist confesses:
*I've been trying to carve*
*a space for myself here*
*to be between*
*softness and strength,*
*to be who I am.*
*But I'm not sure*
*there is such a place—*
*at the king's palace*
*or anywhere else.*

I settle my hand on Franz's.
*You dream of foxes ...*
*but they are more*
*than just their silence.*

*Foxes outlive*
*the wolves and the forest fires.*
*They make a home*
*and a charm of companions*
*wherever they go.*
*You can too.*

But is the same true
of the deer whose death
brought Richter such joy?
Did its soul ever reach
the serenity of the Other Wood—
what should be
its final home?
Or without me, my gift,
my star-touched spells,
is its spirit
left to wander the winds?

Are the deer and I
both trapped
in our seclusion and strangeness
by the acts of a single
             selfish
boy?
             (And his arrows?)

## Chapter Forty

**Franz and I leave the protection of the birch.**
We ramble
around the lake,
putting off our inevitable return
to Richter's castle.

We only stop when we reach
the top of a hill and can go
no further
than the cliff's jagged edge.

Below, the lake watches the world,
singular and blue
as Odin's eye.
Above us, the mountains
Richter calls *the Alps*
cut into the sky like teeth.
And along their green slope
are the woods
made of magic, sisterhood, my past.

(Relief and longing
war within me
as I measure the distance
between myself and the forest.

It is
so far away;
it is
so close.)

Franz stands
where the cliff meets the air,
gazing into the lake.
Do they hope
they can divine the future
from the waves?

What the artist says
is even more surprising
than a guess
about what tomorrow might bring.
*We should jump.*

**I twirl around, laughing.**
*Franz, you can't be serious!*

But the artist's face
is stern as the mountainside.
*We should jump*
*so that when we look back*
*on today,*
*we'll remember*
*some joy, some adventure*
*and not only death.*

*We can't!*
*It's too high.*
> (And I am without
> my wings.)

*Please, Hilde.*
Franz sweeps
their hand across the cloud fields,
as if to twine
the wisps around their fingers.
They are seeking to create
even here, even now.
*You won't get hurt.*
*I won't let you.*
*I promise, Hilde.*

Promises made by mortal lips
are made
to be broken, like the short thread
of their lives.
But Franz was made
for only truth.

I take their hand
and the artist whistles
> the major seventh chords
> > in the key of F.

I answer
with a whistle of my own.

Buoyed by the music,
we march
boldly to the edge of the cliff,
              and
                        we

                                  jump.

It is as close to flying
                    as I've come
                              in months.

**We strike the surface of the lake**
and are lost
in the blue.

Bubbles rise
like fireflies around our smiling mouths.
But Franz and I
don't let go of each other
till we float
up to feel the sun on our faces.

        (What having a friend means:
        never being alone
        in the dark

and laughing
when the shadows break.)

Side by side,
we swim back to the land.
I cut more easily
than any blade through the water.
Franz splashes along beside me,
floating on their back,
crawling on their stomach.

*I should have remembered*
*what a terrible swimmer I am*
*before we jumped,* they gasp.

Now, I make a promise
of my own.
*I won't let you sink.*

And I don't.
        (I never leave
        my promises
        unfilled.)

**Franz Mendelsohn,**
        the lake weeping
                from their long hair,
        laughter dripping
                from the corners of their mouth

is:

       a crown of forget-me-nots,
       a falling star whose soaring light
       I almost hope to meet with my own,
       a nocturne in palest lavender.

They are
entirely themself,
as I haven't been all summer.

I am
       straining
          against
my self-imposed exile, my girlishness.

I need to feel the stardust
knotted in my cloak;
I need the clarity
that comes to me as I ride the wind.
I need to see
if the deer's soul
clings to the groves of trees
it can no longer call home.

I need to use my magic
for my own desires.

## Chapter Forty-One

**Richter's castle is a hearth**
emptied of a flame or kindling;
Franz and I
find no one else here
upon our arrival.

Have Richter and his friends
gone to Munich,
their bellies heavy with venison?
Did they return to the hunt,
hungry for more death?
Wherever they might be,
their absence stirs
sudden unease
in me.

*I'll see you soon,* I tell Franz,
a second promise
to go with my first.

But I'm quick to rush
back to my room
and throw open
my wardrobe's doors,

shoulders aching for my wings
as scar tissue
throbs beneath a veil of rain.

But the wardrobe,
            like the castle,
is empty.

My cloak
            (my *wings*)
is gone.

**I search the stone halls and courtyard**
for Richter and my wings,
my heart
            clawing
up my throat a little more
with each breath I take—
an animal
I can't soothe.

I don't dare
ask Franz for help,
and the sun offers me none;
it hides behind
its own cloud-cape,
refusing to lend me more
than weak gray light.

It isn't until sunset
bloodies the sky
that Richter crosses his threshold.

I throw myself at him,
managing only one
            desperate
            word
at a time.
*Richter,*
*where*
*were*
*you?*
*What*
*happened?*
*Where*
*is*
*my*
*cloak?*

Shadows pool in Richter's gaze,
dead stars consuming
every fleck of fragile light.

But far worse is the bow
notched in his hand,
marking him
for what he is

and what he has been

from the start:

a hunter.

I recognize

his arrow now,

the red tip, the evergreen plume.

I saw it

rising from the boar's belly

on the day

I abandoned sisters, wings, woods.

The boar, the deer, the swan-maiden

far from home:

We were all

Richter's prey.

         And we have all

             been

                 caught.

## Chapter Forty-Two

*I have your cloak,* Richter says.
*But I've hidden it away.*
*You were going to* leave me, *Hilde.*
*I saw it*

*in your eyes—*
*the shape of your forest,*
*the reflection of your sisters,*
*how much time*
*you spend with Mendelsohn*
*and the king's fairy tales.*

He places
a hand on my shoulder,
the weight of stolen wonder
sinking into me.
*I need your magic;*
*I need you.*
*And I can't let you go . . .*
*not until I'm ready.*

Even without wings,
I am faster
than any mortal girl
has the right to be.
I lunge for the boy,
a rage
of red hair and teeth.

I stretch my hands out, ready
          (and eager)
to wrap
sharp fingers around

Richter's white throat
and *squeeze*.

>       (If I can't be a swan,
>       let me be a briar vine;
>       let me be a rose
>       with thorns to spare.)

But before I can touch him,
Richter grabs
my wrists
and I feel
        my bones
threatening to break.
I don't scream—
but I want to.
The pain is enormous,
a country
compressed in the bruises
beginning to stain my skin.

Richter's color rises
at my defiance.
He is strawberry red, all summer fury.
*If you hurt me,*
*you'll never see*
*your cloak again, Hilde.*

*No one else*
*knows where it's hidden.*
*No one else*
*can return it to you ...*
*and I will.*
*But only*
*if you stay with me*
*as long as I want.*

**The boy tightens his grip.**
I feel him, *all* of him,
fever-wild and
   slipping
into
   some
       inner darkness
I don't wish to see.
*Richter—*

*If you try to run,*
*I'll follow your footprints*
*into the mountains,* the boy hisses.
*I'll take you back—*
*no matter how many of your sisters*
*I have to bring down*
*with my arrows*
*to do it.*

Five swans can shatter almost anything
        (be it a finch's eggshell
        or a vulture's wing)
but only if they are prepared
for war.
And my sisters know nothing
of this hunter.

Trapped
in my smallness,
the ordinary life
I sold half my magic for,
I would be powerless
to stop Richter from claiming
        each
        and
        every
        swan
and all the wishes
we call into the world.

My cloak was meant
to protect me,
not used as a means to hold me
prisoner.

But Odin All-Father
should have seen the greed of men

and understood that anything
      (a girl,
      a cloak,
      a pinch of magic)
could become a weapon
in the right hands.

**What I see as night**
falls
like a blade:
a boy,
hungry for and haunted by
the ghosts of the princes
he longs to be.

What I see as night
falls
like the boar did
on the spring day when I rejected
so much of myself:
no choice
but a single choice,
a lonely path
beside Richter
winding back to the clouds
and the strength that was once mine.

      (Strength I didn't fully grasp
      till I no longer had it.)

What I see as night
falls
like my heart and hopes:
a return
to the isolation of my forest—
not only as a knife
to cut souls free
from their aching limbs
but as a warning
and a shield,
protecting my sisters
from Richter and all his desires.

**This must happen to every girl,**
eventually.
None of us are exempt.

We all trust a dangerous boy
at least once—
because he pretended to be sweet,
because he was charming,
because he seemed like a summer storm
we could throw ourselves into
and emerge from, exhilarated
but still intact.

Baron Maximilian von Richter
has never been a storm.

He is a cage—
and now, he has caged *me*.

## Chapter Forty-Three

**Evening descends and as Richter sleeps,**
his dreams
shallow as ever, I tear
through his castle
in search of my cloak.

I channel
the hunger of the wolves,
the cleverness of the ravens,
the silence of the foxes.

I pry
at loose stones on the floor.
I rip
tapestries from the walls.
I open
door after door,
wardrobe after wardrobe.

But the castle denies me
what is mine.

Furious, I scale its walls,
leaping into
the spartan trees beyond
to peer inside
badger dens and broken tree trunks.

I wade
knee-deep into the rivulets
trying to find their way
to the lake.
The water steals
my latest pair of shoes;
I let it, hoping
they will be accepted
as an offering.

I beg, I bargain,
I try to sway the yews
and birches into surrendering
my cloak.
But they refuse to disclose
their secrets
to the likes of me,
the creature who deserted
her own woods—
and a part of herself
in the bargain.

**I abandon my search**
as the sun sweeps over the Alps,
and enter
the castle's meandering halls again.

A door
      BANGS
open at the end of the corridor,
Richter's typical way
of announcing himself.

He shouldn't have bothered.
I memorized the smell of him
long ago.
sandalwood
and midnight deeds.

Richter stalks over to me,
grabbing
at the tatters of my dress.
*What happened to you?*
*Where are your damn shoes?*

I smile,
reveling in the dead leaves
clinging to my hair,
the earth caught between my toes.
It feels forbidden, like a piece of me

I've stolen *back*.
*I lost my shoes.*
*But it's not as if*
*I prefer to walk,*
*now is it?*

Richter's mouth
slams shut
like his multitude of doors.
      (I know Franz would laugh
      if they were here, if they understood
      the punch line to my joke.)

*Get dressed properly,* Richter snaps.
*I have news.*

## Chapter Forty-Four

**Franz, Richter, and I**
      (artist and baron and lady no more)
have received invitations
to a gala
at the only palace Ludwig has completed:
Schloss Linderhof.

I doubt
Ludwig wanted to host this party.

Someone else must have insisted
he see and *be* seen
by the nobility.
There is power in the images
other people build of us
like castles and cloudscapes.
And a king can't appear
springtide soft
in front of his courtiers,
lest his country's borders fall
as easily as his tears.

Richter is quick to snatch
Franz's invitation from their hands,
and glower at it.
*I don't know*
*what the king was thinking,*
*inviting you, Mendelsohn.*
*This gathering*
*should be for nobility alone.*

Richter doesn't look
at Franz
as he speaks;
he looks at *me*,
a message from man to beast:
there is no room in our circle,
            (tight as shackles)
for Franz.

But I've already spent too long
appeasing my captor,
being who and what
he told me *to* be.
Let Richter see me, the *real* me,
as he saw me this morning,
muddied, indelicate, not at all his.

I ask Franz:
*Do you want to go?*

*I don't* not *want to go.*
       (There's a truth in Franz's lie
       and a lie in that truth,
       nested together.)
*But I've never been*
*especially good at dancing.*
The artist twirls
to demonstrate, tipping
to the side.

*Come anyway,* I say.
*Surely someone there*
*can teach you*
*how to dance.*

## Chapter Forty-Five

**Schloss Linderhof**
feels like one of Ludwig's dreams
reconstructed
in the waking world.

Pristine white and gilded with gold,
Schloss Linderhof is all light.
Stone river gods
reign over laughing fountains;
man-made rivers
tumble down the hills.
Flowers
       (not a petal out of place)
bloom in the shapes of stars.
Only a huge linden tree
            disrupts
the symmetry of these gardens.
It grows where
       (and how)
it pleases, in the very heart
of the palace grounds.

I never thought
I'd envy a tree.

I never thought anything with such deep roots
could be more wild
than I am.

**Tonight, Richter cannot keep his hands**
        off
                of
                        me,
his most
prized possession.

My new party dress
is made of moonlight,
and Richter strokes my collar
where the fabric breaks
in cosmic waves
on my shoulders.

*What else could we dream up*
*if we put our minds to it?*
Richter muses so quietly
not even Franz
        (trailing behind us, an afterthought
        to all but me)
can hear him.
*An entire castle?*
*A brand-new country?*

I sweep my fingers
down the dress I'm floating in.
*What else*
*could you dream.*
*None of this*
*is mine.*

Richter kisses
the back of my hand,
my knuckles
roughed from my girlhood adventures—
those he would make sure
I never experience again.
*But it could be.*

**Mila, the harsh girl with the harsher portrait,**
            the one who first told me
            about Franz,
is among the guests tonight.
Her radiance is unblemished.
But something about her
is *different*.

Her words don't prick like talons
against tender hearts.
She invites her sister, Ursula,
into conversations

*(Have you met my sister?*
*She has a singing voice*
*that's marzipan sweet!)*
the other girl
was once excluded from.

It must have been
the truth in Franz's portrait
that made her decide
she needed a new shape, a gentler one;
very few creatures
want to stay cruel.

And I know
        (better than most)
what it's like
for a single piece of art
to change
the course of a life.

**In fire opals and gold leaflets,**
the guests at Ludwig's party
outshine
summer's final sparkle of fireflies.

Richter and I dance beside them,
linden blossoms
raining down on us
like a storm of shooting stars.

But each time
the boy spins me around, I look
to Franz, kneading at their top hat
as they wait to dance.

      (As they wait
      for *me*.)


I want to show Franz how I danced
at my first ball,
like mist gliding
on the water,
my swan's ballet of delight.


As it is, I must close my eyes
      and endure
Richter's hand on my hip,
my fingers latched in his.


      (I must
      bide my time.)

## Chapter Forty-Six


**All enchantments must end,**
for better or for worse.
And this evening's

is smashed to brittle pieces
by Richter.

He sweeps me
to the front of the jubilant crowd,
thrusts
his hands into my hair
as he might stab his knife
into a hapless creature's belly, and
                          kisses
me.

Our second kiss is harsh,
the blistering cold of a midwinter's day,
a word spoken in anger,
          (but never regretted)
a bruise
eclipsing my mouth.

This time,
I don't kiss Richter back.
It doesn't matter;
my silent protest only encourages him
to go even deeper.

          Why won't this boy
                 STOP
          stealing from me?

**My captor breaks the kiss**
as another would break
a wayward heart.
I try to tear myself away—
but there is nowhere
for me to run.

The stone statues watch us
from the sides of the path.
They drink in the scene
as their marble faces
take in rainwater and the ages.

The court is no better.
A few of the young men
       (Richter's fellow thieves
        and hunters)
cheer for him;
the silken ladies giggle
on my behalf.

I want to scream:
*You don't know*
*what this boy has done!*
*You don't know*
*what he still may do*
*if I wipe his scalding kiss*
*off my lips!*

I need to wrench
the right words from my throat.
But before I can,
Richter seizes me and slips
a ring

        onto

                my

                        finger,

just above
the blackberry patch of the bruises
his anger left behind.


Richter and I
didn't make this piece of jewelry
together;
it is all his doing, a silver band
        (noose tight)
that holds a single diamond,
a lonely wish.


Richter grinds
his knuckles into my waist,
shoving me
onward to meet
the blurring faces of the court.
My tongue tries to form
a single cry
        (*Stop stop stop!*)

but it won't obey me
as Richter announces:
*I'm thrilled to tell all of you*
*Hilde and I will be married*
*on the winter solstice!*

He plants another kiss
on my temple like larkspur
and murmurs:
*I've already begun to dream*
*the dress you'll wear*
*before the whole of Bavaria.*

The others hear
the boy's strained attempts
at romance;
I hear a command
grimmer than any soldier's.

**The cage door is closing,**
the lock being fastened.

No arrow to the heart
could be worse
than *this*.
Or so I believe
      until
      I see
      Franz.

Hurt has opened like a moonflower
on their face.
I know
what the artist must think
about the desire
raging in Richter's eyes,
the false engagement
strangling me
before every human
whose life
has ever brushed against mine.

I want to tell Franz:
*It's not like this.*
*It will never be*
*like this.*
*I haven't chosen Richter*
*even if he*
*has chosen me.*

But Richter, adept
at thievery above all else,
steals me away
before I can.

## Chapter Forty-Seven

**I will not give this boy**
a third kiss,
even as he drives me
back into a hedge, intent on claiming
my lips
thrice over.

> (Richter is red-faced and needy;
> I'm pale and vicious.
> We are both
> in our element;
> we are both
> standing in our truths.)

*Richter, stop!* I shout.
*You have magic*
*of your own now.*
*That's what riches and power,*
*charm and grace*
*are in the human world.*
*Hold them close . . .*
*and* let me go.

Richter cups my chin
in his (white) gloved hand, smiling.
(He looks as if
he wants to kiss me.
He looks as if
he wants to open the bars
of his ribs
and stuff me inside.)

*After the wedding,*
*I* will *return your cloak*
*and you can go*
*wherever you like*, he tells me.
*I'll spin*
*a dream of my own,*
*how I was tragically widowed,*
*my bride taken*
*before her time.*
*The court will eat up*
> *my tragedy,*
> *my broken heart,*
> *my first love*
> *withered on the vine.*
*And they'll all*
*love me for it.*

But Richter has crushed
each of his vows to me

under his heel.

If he tires of me,

there is nothing to stop him

from tearing five sister-swans

out of the sky.


I must save

myself and my kin

from the hunter

who has ensnared me;

I must reclaim

all the parts of me

he has cleaved away.


But how?

**Chapter Forty-Eight**


**Richter returns to the party;**

his friends gather him up

in all their splendid glory,

their congratulations puncturing the air.

    *(What a perfect match!*

      *She's so lovely!*

        *We're all so excited*

          *for your future!)*

It is only Franz
who starts toward *me*,
the look in their eyes
a wound,
my name scarring their lips.

But I can explain nothing to them
without the truth . . .
and the truth
is the one piece of me
I'm afraid to place
in anyone's hands again.

The instant
Richter's back is turned,
I run
into the woods encircling the palace.
The trees here are tame,
pruned and trimmed,
planted rather than grown.
But my feet still tap
little prayers on their roots.
Like a ring of salt,
they might protect me.

I beg of them:
*Hide me,*
*swallow me,*

*make sure Richter*
*can never find me again.*

He can't be
my forever,
the first and last chapter of who
I am
supposed to become.

What I find
in place of answers
is a lodge.

**The little lodge**
isn't meant to house hunters.
I understand its purpose
without asking anyone:
This is Ludwig's sanctuary.
It feels like the king,
a story that's wandered
off its pages.

There's no lock on the door;
I didn't expect there to be.
No one else
would want to leave
the majesty of Schloss Linderhof
in favor of the forest.

No one
        but me.
No one
        but Ludwig.

An ash tree
is planted in the lodge's single room.
This could be the same tree
Odin hung from,
its branches
coiling and snarling
like my thoughts.

A sword is embedded
in the ash's trunk,
calling out to be drawn—
and used.
But against which foe?

I'm the monster
in one version of the story,
the unnatural temptress,
the daughter of a god on a tree.

But in another version
        (my own retelling)
I'm the victim,
my power ripped from my hands

and replaced
with the hateful diamond ring
winking at me.

And in Franz's version,
I may be their heartbreak
given breath.

**I'm not alone for long;**
I never am.
The door opens with a groan,
as if the lodge is exhaling
a long-held sigh.

King Ludwig has a talent
for interrupting my solitude.
If he weren't so kind,
if he hadn't brought Franz to Neuschwanstein,
I'd resent him
for this latest intrusion.

*Fräulein Hilde,* Ludwig says.
*I'm not surprised*
*you came here, to Hundinghütte.*
*The lodge seems like a place*
*you might have called home,*
*once.*

I sweep a curtsy.
I'm getting (too) good at this.
Courtly pretending
feels natural now,
as sailing above the tree line
once did.

*Ihre königliche Hoheit.*
*Your Royal Highness.*

Ludwig's eyes move to the sword
I won't pull free.
   (But want to, desperately.)
*Should I offer my congratulations*
*or my condolences*
*on your engagement?*

The tips of my ears burn
and I bite back
a curse
I'd cast on myself.

If I can blush,
I might have finally become
(too) human, my wish
fulfilled.


   (Much to my own sorrow.)

**Ludwig begs me in a starlit voice**
not unlike Franz's:
*If you don't love*
*Baron von Richter,*
*please don't make the same mistake*
*I did,*
*pledging yourself to the wrong person.*
*Only give yourself to someone*
*who understands you.*
*Does the baron?*

*There is someone else*
*in my life*
*who may understand me*
*more than him,* I confess.

But if I tell Franz the truth,
I risk betrayal.
I'll be vulnerable, as I was
with Richter.
And weakness
is a knife to those who know
how to use it.

*Who are you, Fräulein Hilde?*
The question is candid.
But not as blunt
as the one Ludwig is truly asking:
*What* are you?

I guide my hand
along the sword's hilt.
The silver sings
in time with the anger
I've carried all evening.
*I'm the monster waiting*
*at the end of the book*
*to swallow the hero;*
*I'm the last gasp of magic*
*most humans*
*won't ever believe in.*
*But you believe—*
*don't you, Your Royal Highness?*


**Ludwig issues no denial;**
he must have run out of lies
years ago.


He makes his own confession
before me and the ash,
before the starstruck sky
and whatever lives
in its darkness.
*When I was young,*
*I had wings of my own.*
*I gave them up*
*for your Richter's father, the first baron.*
*He promised to love me*

*if I became*
*nothing greater*
*than a boy,*
*nothing less*
*than a king.*

Ludwig sighs.
*And for a time, it felt*
*like he did.*
*I thought his kiss*
*could last forever.*
*I thought a crown*
*would make us both happy.*
*But he asked more and more of me,*
*while I received*
*little in return—*
*except the taste of regret.*
*And when I finally refused*
*his demands for wealth*
*and power, he stole my wings.*

The king, my fellow swan,
traces his hands over his shoulders.
They are naked,
buckling under velvet and expectations.
        (Never his own.)
*Magic only exists for me now*
*in harp strings, lines of print,*

*other people's poetry.*
*It's why*
*I've been trying to crawl*
*back into a story for years.*

*Ludwig nods at me.*
*Life's winter stalks our captors*
*and when our jailers leave us*
*for the Other Wood, the Other City,*
*the Other Kingdom*
*of the dead,*
*we are left alone,*
*the bars of our cages intact.*
*Death changes*
*nothing*
*for us.*
*Our youth is eternal and we remain*
*endless*
*summer people.*
*So guard yourself well, Hilde.*
*There isn't much magic*
*left in this country—*
*or any other.*
*It would be a shame*
*if you were lost, as I was.*
*As I*
*still am.*

## Chapter Forty-Nine

**Richter doesn't pursue another kiss**
on our way back to his castle.
He's had too much wine
and danced too many cotillions
to do more than doze
inside the rumbling carriage.

Franz pretends to sleep themself,
but I catch
the candlelit flicker of their gaze
on me
whenever I dare
to look their way.

I can't become like Ludwig.
haunted by regret.
I *won't*.

Yes, I'm already lost,
already wingless.
But I believe magic
may be able to find me.

Magic like the kind Franz carries
in their colors.

## Chapter Fifty

**Inside my rooms,**
I tear off
my moonlit dress.
I'm afraid
if I wear it another minute,
it might become a *wedding* dress—
Richter's final aviary.

Accompanied by night melodies,
       the cool whisper of the wind,
       the soft cricket orchestras
       hidden in the dew-studded grass,
I go to Franz.

**The artist is sitting at the table**
in the castle's great hall.
They paint
with desperate swiftness,
their brush moving
like the sun across the lake,
brightening each sheet of paper.

Franz gifts me with a smile.
They don't
       (can't, *won't*)

mention the party, the ring, the kiss.
*I didn't realize*
*you were still awake, Hilde.*
*I've started*
*a new project!*
*I'm drawing the sweethearts*
*of the workers at Neuschwanstein.*
They hold up these new sketches
of girls whose hands are warm
with a healing touch,
and ladies in shades of milk and honey,
scythes raised as they harvest
wheat and gold.

*Did the workers tell you*
*what their sweethearts excelled at?* I ask.
*Is that why you painted these women*
*in their triumphs,*
*at their best?*

Franz's brush
stops.
*No.*
*I only tried*
*to make the women and girls*
*lovely.*
*That's what's expected*
*of me and my work,*

*isn't it?*
*Loveliness, always.*

The excuse
sticks
to the roof of Franz's mouth
like black bread.
They're lying . . .
even to themself.

If you spend
enough time in another's company,
a new language grows between you—
a garden of foxgloves and daisies,
jokes and barely healed scars.

This is ours:
the dialect of hidden things.

But tonight, my secrets
flow from me
            like blood
whether I want them to
or not.

## Chapter Fifty-One

**The truth, the one,**
the only:

*Franz, I need your help.*
*Richter stole*
*something from me—*
*a cloak*
*woven by my father.*
*It gives me*
*the swan wings*
*you painted me with.*
*The ones you saw*
*over the top of your easel,*
*from the corner of your eye.*

I don't pause for breath.
If I do,
I won't be able to continue.
My courage will fail me
as the light fails
the closing of the day.

*I'm like you, Franz:*
*someone else's miracle*

*stuffed into too-small bones.*
*I used to change*
*between girl and swan*
*the way I change ball gowns now.*
*All of my five sisters*
*could do the same.*
*They still can, in the distant woods.*
*Every breath*
*I've ever taken*
*expels folklore.*

*I bring the dreams of others*
*to life.*
*It's why Richter drips with jewels;*
*why he wants me*
*to marry him.*
*I'm not human.*
*I never have been;*
*I never will be*
*even if I die*
*in this unchanging body.*

**Franz's smile winks out,**
a flame battered
by the icy wind
that will herald my wedding.
*Is this another*
*of King Ludwig's stories?*

*Or is it a tale*
you *invented?*

I never had to beg Richter to believe
in magic.
He grew up with it,
as the trees
grow up with the sky
and the knowledge their end will come
in either rot or fire.
He felt *entitled* to it.

But Franz has made
no such assumptions
about themself or the world.

I remind the artist:
*On the day we met,*
*you saw who I am,*
*under the satin,*
*under the lies you had been sold*
*by Richter and by me.*
*Why else*
*would you have painted me*
*with wings?*

Franz's eyes turn gray
and lonely,

the same shade
as the endless solitude
(and souls) of the Other Wood.
*The portrait*
*was an expression of your beauty.*
*It had*
*no deeper meaning.*
*We don't live in a fairy tale*
*simply because I paint them,*
*simply because they creep*
          *(wildcat soft)*
*into my dreams.*


**Do you think I'm lying**
*or do you think I'm mad?*
I spit.
Which would I prefer to be:
a girl cruel and capable enough
to come up with such a story,
or a girl lost
in a labyrinth of poetry and myth?
Both are painful assumptions.


I thought I could trust Franz.
I thought they saw me,
the most unadorned me
as I see them . . .
and accepted it.

I was wrong.
Why
am *I always* wrong?

*I don't know*
*what you're truly seeking*
*by telling me this tale,* Franz murmurs.
*But whatever it is,*
*I can't give it to you.*
*I'm sorry, Hilde.*

The artist collects
their tools and papers until
their hands
are overflowing
and they flee—

      from me, the table, our conversation.

I try to call Franz back,
but they

      are

already

      gone.

For all their denials,
Franz is more like me
than they will admit.
The artist sees

the spirit behind the smiles,
just as I saw souls growing
like roses in the ribs of the dying.

And I am done
hiding from the truth—
mine or anyone else's.

### Chapter Fifty-Two

**Midnight arrives and I fly**
down the hallways
on my unsure girl-feet, hoping
the too-lively shadows
will accept me
as one of them.

Richter may be watching;
he's in the very foundations here.
And his ghosts
        (standing like birches,
        pale and vigilant)
may roam the castle grounds.
I must be so quiet
I almost forget to breathe.

Franz's room is unlocked.
I've explored this castle
enough times to know
it only allows Richter
his secrets and his privacy;
everyone else
is exposed.

I crouch
at the foot of the sleeping artist's bed.
I hate skulking in the dark;
I hate seeing Franz thrash
in the gloom.
They never gave me
permission to be here.

But I need to make a miracle
Franz can reach out and touch,
a marvel
the artist can slip into their suitcase
alongside their hometown,
their prayers,
their recollections of a childhood
they must be running from.

It's lucky
I excel
at creating such things.

**What I pull from Franz's dreams:**
a single piano key, slim and white
as my swan's neck,
as the fingers
the artists winds around their paintbrushes,
as the blade
of Richter's hunting knife.

A lonely note
is captured in the dented ivory.
I know it well now.
It's the beginning
        (never the end)
of joy
in the major seventh cord.

### Chapter Fifty-Three

**There's intimacy in memorizing**
a person's routines . . .
and I know all of Franz's.

After they pray,
Franz always sits on the window ledge
overlooking the valley,
legs folded, a bowl of porridge

warming their hands.
This morning
is no exception.

I don't greet Franz.
I set
the (stolen) piano key
on the ledge beside them,
letting it speak *for* me.

Franz drops their spoon;
their jaw obediently follows.
*Hilde,*

    *where*

        *did you*

           *get that ...?*

*Don't you remember?*
*You dreamed it,*
*just last night.*
I wait
for Franz to deny the piano key,
to accuse me of

    theft,

    trickery,

    manipulation.

    (Again.)

They do not.

*I thought I lost this*
*on my travels,* Franz whispers,
holding
the piano key against their heart.

*Maybe you did lose it . . .*
*in* this world, I say.
*But there was another version,*
*the one in your memory.*
*It's much harder*
*to lose* that *one.*
*Franz,*
*who does the key belong to?*
*Why is it*
*so special to you?*

But I (think I)
         already know
the answer.

**It belonged to my sister's piano.**
*I stole it*
*before I left home,*
*prying it free with weary fingers.*
Franz slumps.
They hide behind
the shroud of their hair,
as they hide behind

the summer yellows
and winter whites
of their palette.
*How did you do this, Hilde?*
*How did you make*
*my dream real?*

*The same way anyone*
*does* anything, I reply.
*Through my will;*
*I'm just better at it*
*than a human girl would be.*

*Human,* Franz echoes.
*The one thing*
*you're not.*

**Frustration is no new thing to me.**
But being frustrated
with Franz *is.*
I ask them,
*Why didn't you believe me*
*before?*

Franz shoves their porridge aside.
*I* did *believe you.*
*That was the problem.*
*The heart is a window*

*I can always look through,*
*especially when I paint.*
*But it's so much harder to believe*
*in* something
*than it is to believe*
*in* nothing.

I sweep my skirts under me,
lowering
myself onto the floor.
I don't want to overshadow Franz
the way Richter and his castle
overshadow *me*.
*But magic is a part of me . . .*
*and the world.*
*It must be*
*a part of you, too, Franz.*
*It doesn't make life easier*
*to deny that.*
*I tried to . . . and here I am,*
*stripped of everything*
*except a selfish boy*
*dreaming*
*the summertime of his*
          *(new, sharp)*
*life into being.*

Franz looks away, a sunflower
folding inward
at twilight.

**The flicker of gold around Franz returns,**
a butterfly
I've missed seeing the whole of
each time it passes.

I know
what I have to do.
I know
which question
I need to ask Franz.

To hear someone else's grief
is to agree to carry
the weight of it.
And I
have enough of my own.

But I think of Franz's attempts
to warn me about Richter,
their smiles,
the way we held hands
below the surface of the lake.
I think of a betrayal
that could have been

and wasn't
because Franz was willing to admit
they were wrong.

And so I'll square
my (wingless) shoulders
and let the artist's sadness
roll over me, a river spilling
its banks.

*Please, Franz.*
*Tell me*
*what happened to your sister.*
*Tell me why*
*you didn't want to believe*
*in magic.*

## Chapter Fifty-Four

**I was supposed to be a chapter**
in Golda's grand story, says Franz.
*Instead,*
*I'm the epilogue to it.*

*Golda and I*
*wanted to travel the world.*

She planned to write a song
for each city we visited,
a melody that captured
every new street corner,
cemetery,
market square.
And I would paint
what we saw
so we could carry
more than just the memory
of our journeys.
We'd make beauty
where there was none,
spread joy
when there had been sorrow.

But we didn't have the chance to.
When I left home
to wander,
I left alone.

> (I did too.
> But my sisters
> gather more than cobwebs.
> I do not think
> the same can be said
> of Golda Mendelsohn.)

**I can't plunge into Franz's memories**
with the ease
I can submerge myself
in their dreams.
But their words are vivid . . .
as all scars are.

*The winter I lost Golda*
*was as long as our scarves*
*and as bitter as horseradish.*
*The cold clung*
*to every bone and branch.*

*Golda suggested*
*we go ice-skating*
*at the pond*
*on the other side of the town.*
*The ice*
*shouldn't have been thin;*
*we should have been able*
*to dance on it till spring.*

*We didn't.*

*The ice cracked,*
*opening around Golda's body*
*like the mouth of a wolf.*
*My sister disappeared*
         *so quickly*

*her smile*
*didn't vanish along with her.*

*I*
        *jumped*
            *into the water*
*after Golda.*
*I didn't think;*
*I simply did it.*

        *(All my best decisions*
        *and my worst*
        *are made like that.*
        *Especially those made*
        *for the ones I love.)*

*I sank*
*and my hand*
*found Golda's in the darkness,*
*both of us*
        *falling,*
*both of us*
        *trying*
*to hold on*
*to each other and the sun.*

        *(It was a physical thing,*
        *that darkness.*

*It slammed into me*
*like a fist, harsher*
*than even the cold.)*

*I didn't realize*
*it would be the last time*
*I held*
*any part of my sister.*

***It was our uncle who grabbed me***
*by the waist*
*and pulled me back*
*to the light, to the world, to* life.

*I protested*
*at being rescued.*
*I was supposed to be the* rescuer—
*like Tristan the knight,*
*Tristan the strong.*
*But in the end*
*I was overcome by the water.*

*Magic may be real,*
*but for all its might,*
*for all its glamour,*
*for all its beauty,*
*it didn't give me the strength*
*to save my sister.*

*So I refused to believe in it,*
*even when I felt it*
*on my canvas, in the king ...*
*and in you, Hilde.*

*What good are miracles*
*if they can't preserve*
*the most important things in this world:*
*life and love?*

**The artist bites their knuckles,**
holding back tears
and words alike
for a moment so strained
it *aches.*

*After Golda died,*
*I couldn't stay in the town*
*I'd grown up in.*
*I saw her*
*everywhere.*
*Even*
*when the mirrors were covered,*
*even*
*after she'd been buried.*

*I left*
*to fulfill my half*

*of our shared dream;*
*I left*
*because I couldn't live*
*with the ghost of the future*
*that had died with my sister.*

*I'm so sorry, Franz.*
My apology is poor,
no more soothing than a lie.
Franz and I both
have girl-shaped holes
in us.
And I can't mend theirs
any more
than they can mend mine.

I am not
the All-Father.
I can't weave new hope
from light alone.

## Chapter Fifty-Five

**Franz asks, fawn-earnest:**
*Could you bring Golda back,*
*like you returned*

*the piano key to me?*
*Could you make*
*my dreams of her*
*real?*

I should have expected this question.
(I didn't.)
I should have prepared a better answer
than the one I'm about to give.
(I didn't.)

*The real piano key*
*is still gone, Franz.*
*All I did*
*was breathe life into a dream*
*you had about it,* I explain.
*I could bring a Golda*
*out of your dreams.*
*But her steps, her laughter, her music*
*would be all wrong.*
*You can't contain the whole of anyone*
*in a single dream.*
*She'd scare you; you'd scare her.*
I pause, sighing.
*I'm sorry, Franz.*

**Richter would howl**
if I refused to conjure

any dream for him,
rewarding my defiance
with another blackbird cluster of bruises.
Will Franz?

The artist
opens their arms.
I tense ...
and Franz hugs me tight,
snatching breath and fear
from my lungs.

*You don't have to be sorry, Hilde.*
*Thank you*
*for listening to* me, they whisper.
*Thank you*
*for sharing my sadness*
*when I turned away from yours.*

Franz smells so human:
like wool coats
and roads I haven't traveled.
But I don't recoil.
They are not an arrow
feigning sweetness.

## Chapter Fifty-Six

**Franz releases me slowly.**
*I want to help you.*
*Your cloak must be nearby!*
*Richter couldn't have carried it*
*to some other kingdom.*
*He hates this castle*
      *(I know he does)*
*but he never leaves*
*for long.*
*You and I could search for it again,*
*together.*


Together.


Richter likes to imagine
he and I are intertwined,
no different
from the edelweiss flowers
and the pines.
But the two of us
have never been *together*
in anything we do.
I only fooled myself
into believing

we were.
But could Franz and I be?

*I've searched the entire castle—*
*in the highest towers,*
*behind the tapestries,*
*in every chest and wardrobe,* I say.
*My cloak isn't here.*

Franz folds their hands
over mine, their voice hushed
as a lullaby.
*In stories, every castle*
*has a hidden door*
*in its wall or its belly.*
*And this castle*
*can't be any different.*

**My cloak may be all starlight,**
but I was made for the sun.
It's Franz
who moves with ease in the dark.

The artist walks on their toes
and I follow, fascinated.
*Are you sure*
*your dream wasn't real, Franz?*
*Are you sure*

*you're not a fox*
*the way I'm a swan?*

Franz shrugs.
*I'm only myself.*
*But I'm used to working*
*quietly.*

And they do.

**The castle denies us,**
over and over.
Even the new places
Franz chooses to look
  (under the loose stones
  in the eastern tower,
  in the courtyard well
  teeming with more shadows
  than rainwater)
are dusty, barren,
the very opposite of magic.

The night hours
are injured things, dragging themselves
on to a new day.
But even with our magic
combined,
Franz and I can't hold back the sun
as it sneaks

over the mountains,
and I feel myself
spiraling toward a frenzy.

How many more sunrises
until my wedding?
How many more sunsets
must I be a prisoner?

*How do we* know
*Richter hasn't taken my cloak*
*elsewhere?* I gasp out.
*He could have sent it*
*to a place*
*I've only read about—*
*Shanghai or Bombay,*
*New York or Kyoto.*
*He could have sent it*
*to a place*
*you've wandered through—*
*Berlin or Lviv.*

Franz tries
to hug me again.
        (I stand back, a fae thing
        once more,
            hesitant to be snared.)
*Richter wouldn't do that,* they reassure me.

*He wants*
*everything*
*he believes he owns*
*close to him.*
*You'll be able to fly soon, Hilde.*
*And I'm looking forward*
*to watching you.*

Just as I
deal in dreams,
the artist seems to speak and see
only what is real.
I must believe Franz
is telling me the truth
of my future now.

## Chapter Fifty-Seven

**Summer has finally retired,**
leaving autumn
to walk the world in its place.
Have I really been
in the human world
for so long?
Is my winter wedding
really stalking
closer and closer?

Time escapes me, day by day,
as Franz paints and I
brew dreams
for Richter to glut himself on.
His gold now glitters
more than I ever could
and with every impossible coin
I deliver, Richter leaves
my cage door open
a little further.

*Wander if you will,* he says,
fingers snagging in my hair.
*But wander back to* me.
      (As if I have
      a choice.)

At the end of each day,
I retrieve Franz
from Neuschwanstein Castle
so we can begin
our nighttide hunt
for my wings again.
      (And again.)
      (And again.)

The dark circles
eclipsing Franz's eyes

and the restlessness of my steps
tell tales of our failure.
But our stubbornness
is greater than our defeats.

This evening,
I find the artist
bathed in the deepest purples,
            (*mauve* and *violet*)
perched on their ladder,
their spine
stretched like the horizon line.
Franz is always
                        twisting
themself into different shapes
as they work, making space
for Ludwig's stories
            (the only balms
            to the king's wounded,
            once-wild heart)
on the walls.

I shouldn't pause—
for breath or to admire
Franz's work.
But the mural is a door
to a kinder world
I wish I could walk through.

*How do you manage*
*to paint anything but the truth?* I ask.
*All these tales*
*Ludwig loves so much*
*are lies.*

*But they're not!*
*There's a little truth*
*in each of them.*
*See?*
Franz bounces to their feet,
teetering on the ladder
as Neuschwanstein
rests at the edge of the hillside.
*Tristan and Isolde's love*
*overcame hardships.*
*It filled their lives*
*with beauty.*
*What has greater truth*
*than that?*

(What indeed.)

**Franz puts their brushes aside**
and I lead them
(paint splattered,
hands no doubt aching)
out of Neuschwanstein's gates.

We amble down
the well-trod path, surrounded by
a cathedral, a shul, a universe
of pines.

The artist takes my hand
       (I let them—finally.
       I let Franz do
       so many things
       I won't allow Richter
       to do willingly)
their skin cloud-colored
in contrast
to the darker shade of my own.
The light
pouring from Franz
       (as it did from Tristan,
       cursed and beautiful)
far outshines the aging day.

*You've told me*
*about your world,* I say.
*Your art and your sister,*
*your uncle and your town.*
*Now let me show you*
*a little of mine.*

I veer off the path,
leading Franz
deeper into the trees.

Listening to the hum of bees
and the chatter of the hedgehogs
in the gloaming of the day,
I could imagine
I am back in the woods of my girlhood—
if it weren't for Franz's hand
in mine.

*I hear*
*so many creatures*
*and so much song,* Franz sighs,
*I never noticed before!*
*Or have these pines*
*only come alive*
*for you, Hilde?*

I grin.
*All woods*
            *(no matter how small)*
*are lively, if you know*
*how to listen.*

**Wildflowers teasing our ankles,**
Franz leans in and whispers:

*Last night,*
*I dreamed*
*I was a fox again.*
*But this time,*
*I was running at your side.*
*I dreamed*
*I was so fast that I almost flew*
*through the woods—*
your *woods.*

*I was like you and your sisters,*
*able to be human*
*and something else,*
*something* magical.
*Departed souls*
*whorled around me*
*and I helped you*
*usher them into the World*
*to Come.*
*I woke up disappointed*
*it was only a dream.*

I wish,

      I wish,

           I wish

that Franz and I truly were
a new Wild Hunt.
We could share the seasons

        (winters so cold
        they stung,
        springs long as ballads)
and our memories
of the spirits we guided
with one another.

But the artist is human, locked in
a single set of bones,
the silver road
hidden from them.

And if
        (*when*)
I find my cloak, I cannot stay
beside Franz and travel
to cities of lions, cities eternal with them.

To protect my sisters
        from Richter and his greed,
I must return
to the melancholy safety of my woods
        (where six swans
        may one day be forced
        to go to war
        against one ruthless boy)
and the tasks
waiting for me there.

## Chapter Fifty-Eight

**Our birch tree is waiting for us.**
Franz and I dare
to linger under its arms, even knowing
winter is approaching
and Richter would surely be angry
at our lateness, our closeness
if we were discovered.

Franz hasn't
        unbraided
our fingers
yet.
        (I don't want them to.)
Gently, the artist
fans the flames
of my red hair
back from my face.

*Hilde ...*
Franz's breath
        hitches
around things
        unspoken.
*Hilde,*
*I'd like to kiss you.*

It's been ages
since anyone asked my permission,
treated me like a sovereign nation
and not something
to be owned and conquered.

It makes my own confession
easy.
*And I'd like to kiss* you
*in return.*

**I've never tasted summer**
distilled
on my tongue.
But Franz's kiss is warm and slow;
in it there are days
full of flowers
and forever-afters.

My answering kiss
is hotter, sharper.
If I held myself against Franz
for too long,
I would leave blisters
across their pink mouth.

Love should never compress you
so that you will fit inside
        a castle,
                a gown,
                        the palm of a single boy's hand.


Love should make you feel expansive,
a sky of a girl,
a painting
growing in scope
with each new figure and color.


And that is how
I feel with Franz now,
their arms around my waist,
their chin tucked
between my shoulders.


I believe the crow from my childhood
was right:
beside the artist,
I may be more
than just myself.

THE FOURTH TALE

THE FOX IN THE WOODS

### Chapter Fifty-Nine

**There are seven twilights left**
before my wedding.
And there are no less
than seven places in Richter's castle
left unexplored by Franz and me,
corners too well hidden
by night's many hues
for us to search them
in the ebbing red
of a candle alone.

Under the bloodshot eye
of the late autumn sun, Franz tells me:
*If you can keep Richter occupied*
*in the daylight hours,*
*I can search for your cloak*
*one last time.*

*It's dangerous*
*to try to fool Richter.*
I feel as if one of my sisters
      (Rota, pragmatic as a stone;
      Mist, cautious as a deer)
has crept into my mouth
and is speaking through me.
*If he*
*discovers you . . .*

*I'll be careful.*
*If it's here,*
*I'll find your cloak.*
Franz sneaks a kiss
so quick
I could mistake it for wings
caressing my cheek.

I turn
my own head to brush
my lips against theirs,
the feel of the kiss

           dizzying.

Half of me
      (swan and storm)
wants to forget I ever learned
how to kiss a human

when most
have only brought me suffering.

The other half
       (girl and soon-to-be baroness,
         if I am not careful)
wants to be suspended
in this second
and never leave.

I am divided
between love and magic.

**Our kiss is broken**
by the familiar
           SLAM
of boots against the stones
as Richter
swoops into the hallway.
He carries himself
like an ill-omen, a prophecy
yet to be fulfilled.

*Come, Hilde.*
Richter crooks
his fingers at me, as if I am no more
than a dog
he can summon at will.

*We must be fitted*
*for our wedding attire.*

There is
no seamstress or cloth merchant
in the castle,
no one to sew us new finery.
A dream
must be what Richter craves ...
and for once I am happy
to give it to him.

There is no time to whisper
             or plot
with Franz.
I meet the artist's gaze and hope
their gift
allows them to read
the desperate truth
in my spring-touched eyes:
*This is our last chance;*
*use the daylight well.*

**In his rooms,**
besieged by the riches of his world,
Richter dreams us both December's fierceness.

His new cloak is a shimmer
of hoarfrost;
his shoes are black ice.
I am confined to
a gown of icicles,
an aurora caught in them.
I am
a bride of bone,
a bride of the sun's slow death.

When I've finished wringing
his wedding-day dreams
from his mind,
Richter kisses
the sharp bridge of my collarbone,
his smile a sickle
tucked against my throat.
*You are still*
*so extraordinary.*

I hide my scream
in the back of my throat and force myself
to smile.

## Chapter Sixty

**I leave my room to meet Franz**
well after midnight settles its dark mantle
over the castle.
And even then,
I don't feel safe.

(I can't, here.)

It isn't until I press my ear
against Richter's door
and hear
the tired whistle of his breath
that my heart
                stops
its corvid shrieking.

Franz is waiting for me
at the end of the hall.
The shadows paint them
a cool midnight blue.
After Richter's fevered touches,
it's a relief
when the artist's arms
enfold me.

*Did you find my cloak?*
*Or even a hint of it?*
*Please tell me*
*you found*
something.

But when I look
into Franz's eyes,
they are haunted by something
                        darker
than the sunstruck phantom
of their sister.
*Hilde, you* must *leave*
*this castle*
*tonight.*
*It's too dangerous*
*for you to stay.*

**I shake myself free,**
passing through Franz's hands
like rain.
*Franz, no!*
*I can't leave.*
*Not until*
*I've found my cloak.*
*Not until*
*I can protect my sisters.*
*Not until*
*I'm my whole self again.*

Franz cups my face
in their hands.
*You're already yourself, Hilde.*
*You could never*
*be less than that.*
*You don't need*
*your cloak.*
*I see you—*
*all of you.*
*Your light,*
*the depths of your magic.*
*You could make yourself*
*into anything—*

        *a bend in a rainbow,*

        *a gust of wind,*

        *a summer day,*

        *a swan—*

*with a wave of your hand.*


*Without my cloak,*
*I don't have*
*that kind of power,* I snap.

        (Am I trying to prove Franz right

        and show them I'm still a swan,

        savage to the last?)

*All the magic in me*
*belongs to someone else—*
*it always has;*

*first Odin, now Richter.*
*What has made you*
*so afraid?*

Franz's confession
is petal-soft.
*I'm not afraid*
*of what Richter might do to me.*
*I'm afraid of what he could do*
*to you.*
*Knowing what's hidden*
*in this castle*
*won't give you back*
*what you've lost, Hilde.*
*It won't change your life*
*for the better.*
*It will only haunt you,*
*as the dead*
*and all the futures*
*they take into the ground do.*

But I'm no willow,
easily swayed by another.
*If the choice*
*is to know the truth*
*or to be safe,*
*I choose to know, Franz.*

*I've had my fill*
*of secrets.*
*Show me*
*what you've found.*

## Chapter Sixty-One

**Franz takes me**
to a forgotten part of the castle,
ruled by dust and cobwebs.

A pass of the artist's nimble hands
along the right stones
forces a sagging wall to cave
                            inward.
A staircase slithers deep,
                    deep
inside
the castle's belly,
this strange extension of Richter's body
and his family line.

I follow Franz's descent,
listening (unwillingly) to the history
caught like a choked breath
in the damp air.

*This is no place*
*for something with the roots*
*of ash trees*
*in place of veins,* the stale breeze whispers.
*Leave, leave, leave.*
*Turn away*
            *before*
                      *it's too late.*

In my head,
the voices sound like the final pleas
my sisters made
before they left me in the Marienplatz.
            (And before I
            left them.)
The weight of the worry and the fear
sticking to Franz
drags my own feet down.

I
            persist
anyway.
I have to.

**The stairs stop abruptly.**
But that's true of any ending.

The cellar is cool, an eternal autumn
trapped below the earth.
I fight back a shiver.
Now is not the time
to show weakness—
however small, however slight.

Franz holds their candle high
and light splashes on the walls.
*I'm sorry, Hilde.*
*I'm sorry*
*for all of this.*

In the gloom,
I see
what Franz has fought
to keep hidden.

All around me are:
sealskin coats
          with no one to wear them,
stag antlers
          without a proud head to crown,
sparrow wings and swan wings
                    (not mine)
          with no one to make them beat.

These creatures
            (long gone)
are my kin
by soul
            (half and half,
            this and that)
and circumstance.
They, too, must have been locked
in this castle, endlessly bleeding
magic
for its residents.

Did the Richter family imprison
their seal girls, stag boys, winged things
with wedding rings?
Or did they simply bury them
after their magic
            (and obedience)
ran dry?

I see the answer
to my question
in the scratch marks on the walls,
the splintered feathers,
the blood dried to black
on the stolen wings and pelts.

The defiance of these creatures
must have been the last mark
they made
on this world—
all except for Ludwig,
the king in his golden cage.

Because the single pair
of swan wings,
their sparkling plumes, their loneliness,
must belong to *him*.

**Franz waves the shuddering candle**
over the relics
Richter's ancestors
must have prayed for and to.

*When I saw these, I realized*
*you weren't the first myth*
*Richter's family hunted down.*
*These people*
*take and take and* take
*whatever they want*
*from the forest.*
*And they don't care*
*how much hurt they cause.*
*Hilde, please.*
*We need to go back,* Franz begs.

*Before*
*it's too late.*

The artist finds my hand
in the darkness.
But I find
no comfort in it.

I believe it may be
too late already.

## Chapter Sixty-Two

**We rise from the cellar**
one stair at a time,
pursued
by the candle's sickly glow.

Each step
allows me to put the feathers and pelts
      farther
      and
      farther
behind
and beneath me.
But above me,

a gale rattles the castle walls,
mimicking my trembling hands.

*I have to find my cloak,*
*I have to, I chant.*
*I can't stay here,*
*being nothing*
*but Richter's creature, watching him*
*rob the world of magic.*

*You don't need to, says Franz.*
*You are*
*maid and fairy tale,*
*girl and other.*
*Cloak or no cloak,*
*you'll always have*
*yourself, your power.*
*And*
                    *(if you want)*
*you'll have me, too.*
*Together, we can warn*
*your sisters about Richter,*
*protect them should he ever*
*try to invade your woods.*
*Together, I believe*
*we can change our tomorrows*
*for the better.*

**I recoil from Franz.**
I've heard these words before
from Richter
> (his smirk
>
> cutting to the bone)
and foolishly pressed them
like wildflowers
into the caverns of my heart.

Any oath Franz
> (no Tristan,
>
> no true prince or princess
>
> in armor dazzling as the dawn)
makes
to shield me from harm
is just another lie, another trap,
another false hope.

Anger scalds my vision, burning
its edges.
*Don't tell me to abandon myself*
*and my strength*
*when you can't protect me!*
*You can barely protect*
*yourself!*

*I could try to—*
*if only you would let me,*

*if only you would* trust *me.*
Franz's side locks
scrape at their cheeks
as they shake their head.
*I won't force you*
*to leave.*
*But I*

      *love you,*

          *Hilde.*
*I don't want to see you*
*down in the cellar,*
*a stolen myth, proof of a conquest.*
*You deserve*
*so much more than that.*


*Your love won't save me,* I snarl.
*It can't.*
*You're just like Richter,*
*telling me*
*where to go and what to do,*
*making oaths you're bound*
*to break.*
I point to the oak doors
leading to the lake, the Alps,
the cities stationed
past their summits,
my hands quivering more than ever.
*If you won't help me*

*take back*
*what's mine,*
*then take your things,*
*take your love,*
*and*
*GET*
*OUT.*

The tears in Franz's eyes
are the closest I'll ever come
to catching the stars
now that I've been denied
the sky.
*Maybe my love*
*can't save you ...*
*but I don't want you to be*
*alone.*

I choke on the bitterness
born from Odin's gift
and my days
in this haggard castle.
*I am always*
*alone, even in your company.*
*I will always be*
*alone, even after I return*
*to my sisters.*

(And I was a fool to think
one artist, the thread of their life
stained-glass fragile,
could change that.)

**Franz disappears from my sight**
like too many souls have before:
lifted by
the wind and their coattails.

But they do not drag me
after them—
by hair, by hand, by heart.
They allow me that much freedom
at least.

## Chapter Sixty-Three

**The snow begins to fall**
the moment Franz escapes
Richter's castle and all their ties—
to me,
to the king,
to the murals
on the walls of Neuschwanstein.

Maybe by banishing Franz,
        keeper of a hundred hues,
        keeper of all brilliant things,
I summoned
the full force of winter.
I walk into the gathering snow
as the sun
(finally) climbs over the valley.
The storm swirls around me,
not unlike
a wedding veil.

I should be used to being
        Hilde,
        the lost and the lonely.
I have been just that
for such a long time.
But I wanted to be
so much *more*.

I look to the white wastes,
searching for signs of Franz—
a scratch of rose-dust pink,
viridian green,
dandelion yellow.
I want to see them again.
        (And I don't.)

Were they right?
Could I call back my wings
if I tried?

I raise my arms
until they ache
with the cold
and heaviness of my (broken) hopes.

In the end, they're useless
for everything
except holding someone
who isn't here.

**Richter's temper erupts**
when he wakes and realizes
Franz is gone.

He tears the artist's remaining sketches
            (impersonal,
                containing no images of love
            or magic)
to pieces,
scattering their fragments
as if they, too, were snowflakes.

*How dare Mendelsohn do this
to me?* Richter roars

at the heart of this blizzard,
his face
plum-colored.
*The king himself*
*hired that artist*
*and now I'll be blamed*
*for driving Mendelsohn away!*

He stomps his feet
like a child.
Our breakfast dishes
       (the stuff of Richter's dreams—
       porcelain and silver,
       studded with gems)
jump.

I watch his tantrum
through half-lidded eyes.
My face is stone.
       (If only
       my heart was too.)
*Maybe some people*
*aren't meant to be tied*
*to any one place,* I say.
*Maybe some of us*
*are meant to be free*
*and to do as we please.*

Richter scowls,
knowing I'm no longer speaking
about Franz.
*Oh,*

   *shut*

*UP,*

   *Hilde.*

## Chapter Sixty-Four

**Eager to slip away**
from Richter's boyish wrath,
I climb the hill to Neuschwanstein.

In the artist's absence,
the place is a lonely den.
No number of picture frames
inlaid with gold
or silk curtains
can warm it.
It lost the person who gave it
a heartbeat of its own.

I don't intend on returning
to the king's half-finished bedchamber,
but that is where my footsteps
carry me.

Franz, too, must have come here
        (after I cast them out
        of my life and this valley)
and draped a cloth over the mural
they worked on throughout
our long, long summer.

I grab the corner of the cloth
and rip it down.
It beats at the air
        (a false pair of wings)
before floating into my
        (limp)
hands.

Laughter and tears
go to war in my throat.
I can't fall apart now.
I must be steel, not a glass princess
about to shatter.

But how can I be strong,
when Franz's last act here
was to paint over their original mural
        and paint
                the two of us
        in its place?

**We are Tristan and Isolde.**
We are as we were
on the night I shared
the forest with Franz
and we shared
our first kiss.

My painted self
sits in the ring
formed by the artist's arms,
my fingers weaving
through Franz's dark curls,
their lips brushing my temples.
Around us,
bellflowers nod their acceptance
of our presence
and our love.

I fall back,
eyes burning like embers.
Even far from any sea,
I can taste salt
    (sorrowful,
       full of exiled things)
in the back of my throat.
I could still run to Franz
and take them to my woods.
We could arm ourselves

against Richter's wrath.
We could—

I try to shake this weakness
aside.
A painting
is just a painting
and I am no Isolde, facing my doom
with a knight at my side.

I have been stripped of everything
but myself.

### Chapter Sixty-Five

Searching for my cloak
in the last six twilights
leading up to my wedding,
I destroy:

Two red velvet coats,
the seams torn apart, thread by thread.

One satin top hat,
stomped on with dagger heels.

A wardrobe,
the doors ripped off,
the wood battered by my fists.

My nails
when the walls wouldn't give.

My battered heart,
or what is left of it.

**On the morning of my wedding,**
Richter's voice
tears me from the blue
      (Berlin or robin's egg,
        I don't know)
haze of my misery.

He speaks in threes
      (*Hilde, Hilde, Hilde*)
as any witch would,
and I raise
my head.

In these long moments before sunrise,
the boy is
      (as ever)
framed by the darkness.
*It's time*, Richter says.

## A Warning About Swans

*Time to show the world*
*what a fine pair we make.*

He and I are quiet as we dress
in our dream-clothes.
He helps button
the back of my gown, his breath
gushing over me
as he arranges frost crystals
along the lean ridges
of my shoulders.

My captor
thrusts his arm out
for me to take.
I don't twine myself around him . . .
but I do pull Richter
            lover-close,
crushing his high collar
in my fist.

*I've seen the last*
*of your secrets, Richter.*
*I've seen what's inside*
*your castle's wide belly.*
*You and your family*
*are nothing*
*but thieves.*

*Everything you have, you stole*
*from some other creature*
*more worthy*
*than any of you.*

Richter doesn't retreat.
Why should he?
He has nothing to fear
from my snapping teeth
and the words
I've polished to a killing edge
as he says:
*I have a wedding gift*
*for you, Hilde.*
*The gift I promised you*
*when I proposed.*

The boy dips a hand
into his jacket,
trimmed with January's frosty kiss.
*I believe* this
            *belongs*
                    *to you.*
Richter withdraws a vial,
small and gray
as a sigh
and pours its contents,

a whisper
of ashes,
into my hands.

This can't be mine;
this can't be meant
for me.
Unless—

Unless.

## Chapter Sixty-Six

**Richter speaks with dreadful care.**
*Now I've kept my promise, Hilde.*
*This is your cloak . . .*
*or what is left of it.*
*On the day I stole it,*
*I burned it, bottled it, saved it as proof.*
*I couldn't risk you leaving.*
*I couldn't risk you leaving me.*

The boy's fingers
uproot strands of my hair like hyacinths.
*I tried to be kind, Hilde.*
*I tried to give you*

*a life, a dream*
*we could share.*
*But*
           *you*
                   *wouldn't listen.*

**Breath and words**
flee my lungs
and my legs give way.

I could scream,
but no one
would hear me.
I could run,
but I have no one
to run *toward*.

I'm trapped
in now, tomorrow, yesterday.
I'm a fixed point, unable
to change.

If Richter
didn't catch me
with hands as gentle as fire,
my descent
           might last
                   forever.

*Now come,*
*we have a wedding to attend.*
Richter's breath reeks, like spilled blood.
          (And the willingness to have more
          on his hands.)
*And if you refuse,*
*I will bring you the heads*
*of five sister-swans*
*by the next full moon.*
*Now*

          *walk*

                    *with me.*


Ash entombed
under my fingernails
and in the valleys of my palms,
somehow,

          I

do.

### Chapter Sixty-Seven


**I remember little about my own wedding**
at the Frauenkirche in Munich,
beneath the marble eaves
and barren eyes of the wooden saints.

I remember little about the vows
torn from my numb lips,
the toasts to health and happiness
crashing over me in cold waves,
the foul taste
of Richter's fourth, searing kiss.

I remember little about the waltz
he and I must have danced to—
two for sorrow, never for joy.

I remember little, except
the blackened, bruised look
in King Ludwig's eyes,
a cracked
        and tilted
mirror
of my own.

We are witnesses
to the downfall of the other ...
and of magic itself.

## Chapter Sixty-Eight

**Our carriage clatters and creaks**
its way back to Richter's castle—
my last resting place
and the grave
of so many others.

Ever the false gentleman,
Richter helps me from the carriage.
He guides me
through the snow
laying siege to the valley,
and back inside his rotten home.

The wind screams,
grieving openly as I can't,
but Richter speaks above it.
*There are firebirds in Kyiv,*
*unicorns roaming the forests of England.*
*You want magic, Hilde?*
*I will give us both better enchantments*
*than your cloak*
*and the adventure*
*of a lifetime.*

I lift my face to Richter's
       (the boy a bullet
       barely contained)
the way I did when I sought a kiss
from someone else.
       (Someone
       I will never be with
       again.)

But in losing everything, I suddenly
see
       it
             all.

When a fire has finished
razing a forest,
when every tree has been reduced
to memory,
when there is nothing left to destroy,
only then
can the wolves find their mates,
and alpine roses blossom from the soil
made rich by the deaths
of elms and alders.

Without Franz, my sisters,
star-spun magic to call my own,
I have nothing left to lose—

except
whatever small part of me
I've managed to hold on to
with bloodied fingertips.

And Richter will have to kill me
to take *that*.

*You believe you own me*
           *(all of me)*
*because of the ring*
*on my finger,* I say to Richter.
*But you don't.*
*Every animal I will ever encounter*
*is my kindred;*
*every river is a song that will accompany*
*the music of my steps.*
*Without you,*
*I am still* me.
*But without me,*
*what are you, Richter?*
*A lonely little boy*
*with no love and no power.*
*Your heart grows roots*
*for no one.*

Richter's lower lip trembles.
I've never seen
tears of rage before,

(they do not fall

peony red as I expected)
but I can't deny
their presence in this boy's eyes.
I've dug my fingers, my words, my *ire*

(and perhaps

my own grave)
into his wounds—
both the old and the new.

*You think*
*you are so special!* Richter hisses.
*But you are disposable!*
*A monster*
*in a modern age*
*that no longer believes in you!*
*If you disappear now,*
*no human being*
*will think to look for you*
*other than in the pages*
*of childhood fables.*

But Richter is wrong.
For all our differences,
my sisters tried to bring me
home.
And there was someone else
who would have searched for me.

That is,
if I hadn't sent them into exile
already.

**Richter crushes me against him.**
In his tearstained eyes, I see
his ravenous hunger.
He may hate me
          (as surely as I hate him)
but he longs to kiss me again.
          (And again.)

*If you want to be a bird*
*so badly,*
*I can grant*
*at least half your wish,* Richter seethes.
*You'll be my prisoner,*
*this castle a cage you'll never leave,*
*until I've wrung*

          *every*

          *last*

          *drop*

*of magic from you.*
He stabs
his finger at the bow
and quiver of red-plumed arrows
mounted on the wall—

a trophy, a threat.
*And if you ever manage*
*to escape,*
*I will find your sisters.*
*One swan girl*
*is as good as the next.*
*I can go through all six of you*
*if I have to.*
*God knows*
*my ancestors did.*

**I feel the strands**
of this place's magic
      (green and jealous)
suddenly
      snap.

The castle doors
      BURST
open
and Richter and I pivot, dragging
each other
toward the wind.

Illuminated by the blizzard,
white as lightning,
      is

              Franz.

## Chapter Sixty-Nine

**Try as I might, I can't speak.**
Did I conjure Franz?
Did I will the artist
off a train, out of a carriage?
Did I pluck them from another land
and drop them at the castle gates?
Franz can't be here ...

                yet they are.


The artist
crosses the threshold, bringing the storm
on their heels
and in the clashing syllables
of the command they give.
*Get*

          *away*
*from her,*

          *Richter!*


I'd forgotten how foxes

          (and the humans

             who resemble them)
have teeth too;
Franz has kept theirs

carefully
hidden, to be used
only in moments of great need.
　　　　(Like this one.)

Richter
　　　　tightens
his grip on me,
invoking
a gasp from me like a prayer.
Are all men in this country
made of iron
and fairy tales?
*Or*
　　　　*what, Mendelsohn?*
He sneers.
*What*
　　　　*can* you
*do*
　　　　*to* me?

**Richter's gaze shifts from me**
for a single moment.
But a moment
can be precious;
and a moment
is all I need.

I have no claws
       (not anymore)
but my shoes
       (pearl buttoned,
         all false innocence)
are just as sharp.
I drive
my heel
into Richter's toes.
He cries out
and I fling myself
from his arms.

This time, it's Franz
who catches me.

The feeling of *belonging*
sweeps me up
as they hold me, tender
where Richter was harsh.

I'm a key
who has found the right lock;
I'm a ship
who has found the right shore.
This *is* forever,
if forever can be another.

(And I believe
it can.)

*I couldn't stay away,* says Franz.
*I couldn't leave you*
*knowing*
*you weren't safe.*

**Richter tears his bow**
off the wall, notching an arrow
against the string
with the same care
as Franz
holds their paintbrushes.

He, too,
reshapes the world
to his liking.
But he is a different sort of artist,
creating pain
where there was none before.

Richter shrieks:
*You are mine, Hilde!*
*This night and all nights,*
*you belong to me!*
The boy
pulls

his drawstring back, a ghoulish smile
suspended in the air,
and the arrow
       flies
             as I cannot.

Despite everything I've given him,
Richter is still
a human boy.
He shouldn't be
this *fast*—
and I wait
for the bite of the arrow's tip.

It doesn't come.
It won't *ever* come.

Because the arrow
       STRIKES
Franz's side
as they throw
       themself
in
       its path.

Blood
       blooms
from Franz's broken skin
like a storm of roses.

And

I

scream.

## Chapter Seventy

**In this burst of blood and flowers,**
I see the future.

I see the world
          (my world)
stained gray,
a world without Franz and magic
for me to protect
and be protected *by*.

I see five more pairs
of swan wings
decaying in this castle.

I see Richter
with everything he has ever wanted,
and nothing he deserves.

What roars to life in me
as Franz spirals toward their death
is not gentle.

It's thunder, full of arrivals.
       (Not departures.)

If Franz is a juniper berry,
I'll be the thorns
shielding them.

If they are a pond,
I'll be the swan
floating on their calm waters.

If they are a palace,
I'll be the myth
roaming through the rooms.

If they are a song,
I'll be the instrument
their notes are played on.

If Franz is wholly themself,
I will be wholly *myself*
and break free of the form
holding me on Earth.

**My girl self**
does not fall away gently.
My swan self
does not emerge with a soft rustle of wings.

My magic
      (mine and mine alone)
          EXPLODES
in blazing color—
dawn and dusk merging into one.

My power is *mine*,
unbound by threads and fathers.
I am
(re)born of my own strength.

**Richter has seen me in flight**
and ground down
beneath his temper and fists.
He has never seen me
in battle.
Now, he will.

I batter
the hunter's face with my wings,
and bruises
erupt like fireworks
on Richter's high cheekbones.
He drops his bow
under my onslaught,
and my claws seek his eyes
before the boy
comes to his senses

and throws

       his arms

              up.

I slice deep

red ribbons across his skin,

but Richter

doesn't emerge from the fight

a blind boy.

I fall back

as a girl, moving with ease on the stones

before I become

a torrent of feathers again.

I cycle—

girl to bird,

flesh to myth

and over again.

But regardless of my shape,

my wrath

is constant.

It leaps from my throat

in avian hisses

and curses uttered

in a half dozen tongues.

*How!*

*How!*

*How!* Richter cries.
He racks his hands
through his hair,
no longer handsome,
only broken.
*I destroyed your cloak!*
*This*
*is*
*impossible!*

My captor
      (no more
      and never again)
collapses on the floor,
his fingers scrambling
over stones as damp
as eyes
on the verge of tears.

Do those same stones
push the bow and quiver of arrows
back into Richter's hands?
I think they must.
This castle is too much his;
staying here
is to invite my own death
and Franz's, too.

To save us both,
I have to abandon the artist.
To save us both,
I have to leave—
and without a single farewell.

I soar
out the door and into
the waiting night.

I'm sorry, Franz.
I'm so sorry.

## Chapter Seventy-One

**I don't settle on any one shape.**
I let the forest floor
drink from both bloodied feet
and wings.

The further I run,
the faster I go,
the more Richter rages.
Somewhere between me,
the shrine made by the pines
        (sacred and dark)

and the eye of the moon
                    (leering and untrustworthy)
he shrieks my name,
                    flaying
                                        open
                                                        the air
with his awful longing.


But I don't conceal
the whistle of breath in my throat
or the symphony of my steps.


Richter needs to chase me;
I need to lead him on—
away from his castle,
to a place
his bloodline does not own.


The appetites of men
                    (of *boys*)
like Richter
are enormous.
But they should fear
the hunger of the dark.
They should know
it's far greater
than even theirs.

**Richter and I have circled back**
to our beginning;
I'd recognize the strawberry patch
we stumble into
anywhere.
Stars and shadows refuse to fall
among these vines
and the heart-shaped berries.

The bones of the boar
are untouched.
They've been waiting
        (for us)
through summer and autumn,
through each change
my captor and I have undergone.

This is where I became
a new creature
of contradictions,
powerless and strong,
liminal and grounded.

This is where I lost
        everything
and found
        something
            (someone)
different in myself.

**Richter ensnares me by the waist.**
His hands scorch me;
they could reduce me to cinders.

*You're mine!* Richter shrieks,
ripping
at my hair, my dress,
every part of me
his grasping fingers
can grasp.
*You'll always be mine!*

The boy would sink
his teeth into me
to keep me *his*,
to keep me pinned on the ground.
He would drag us both
to the Other Wood
            (and further still)
if only
he could continue to own me.

But Franz was right.
I belong
            (first and foremost,
            tonight and always)
to *myself*.
And there is no stronger magic
than refusal.

*No!* I shout.
*No!*
I pool every ounce
of myself, my wings, my heart,
in my open palms
and shove
       Richter
           backward.

The boar's gleaming tusks

                    catch the boy

as
he

                falls,

piercing
through his chest
and the bars of his ribs.

*Hilde,* **Richter coughs**
through the sea of blood
running from his mouth.
*Hilde, please.*
He reaches for me—
to caress me,
to strike me?
I don't know
and I doubt he does either.

(He's never been able
to tell the difference.)

I snarl down at him.
My fury is more than just my own—
I'm seal girls and sparrow girls,
wolf girls and stag boys,
swan after swan.
I'm centuries
of raging magic
and restless bones.
*You forgot*
*your father's warning, Richter.*
*Swans are not delicate.*
*We've never been made of frost;*
*our wings aren't made of glass.*

*Hilde ... please!*
Richter's tears
are far more brilliant
than any word
he's ever uttered.

This boy's wish was
          (is)
to be
          beloved,
                    known,
                              *remembered.*

But I'll grant
its inverse.
He's alone now,
and history
       (and the forest)
will bury
whatever is left of him,
the way he threatened
to bury *me*.

**I'm not a liberator tonight;**
I'm not a silver needle
that will stitch Richter's wound
closed.

It's too late to save him
       (body or soul)
anyway.
Richter is dying;
I'm only here
to see that death through.
I'm the warden,
I'm the executioner,
I'm the blade
carrying out the sentence.

I curl
my fingers

into claws
    and *tear*
        Richter's soul
from his crumbling body.

It burns
against the tips of my fingers,
a tangle of stinging nettle,
a snarling mass of boy
and hate.

Then I toss his spirit
into the air, discarding it
as Richter and his family
discarded so many others.

Let him land
where he lands.
Let him haunt
whatever he haunts.

Richter is done
with me.

    And I

        am done

           with him.

## Chapter Seventy-Two

**The moon**
       (strawberry red,
        swollen with terror)
and the silver road
arching above me
lead me back to the castle.
But I fear
by the time I reach Franz,
they will be
just another gossamer soul
for me to carry.

I soar faster than ever before,
ignoring the cold,
my throbbing wings,
the tears
I've held back
for so long.

I come back to my girl self
at the threshold of the castle
and run
to Franz's crumpled form.
*Franz!*

*Franz,*
*answer me!*

The artist's eyes flutter open,
their lashes and skin
moth gray.
*Hilde.*
*This time, it's you*
*who came back*
*for* me.

I place my hands
on Franz's side.
My fingers come away
drenched in blood,
warm as the single summer
Franz and I spent
in each other's lives.
          (And arms.)
*Of course I came back*
*for you.*
*I wouldn't leave you here—*
*the same way*
*you didn't leave* me.

Franz's smile
is as impossible
as I am.

*I want you to know*
*I'm not sorry*
*I came here.*
*I'm not sorry*
*I met you.*
*I have no regrets.*
*You accepted*
*my true self...*
*and I'm grateful.*

*As a child, my uncle told me*
*heaven is a lake of birds,*
*where each soul*
*has wings of its own.*
*So I know*
*we'll meet again,*
*in some way,*
*in some shape,*
*in some other world.*

**I can't save Franz**
as they are now,
so human and fragile.
I don't have the power
to undo Richter's malice
and the violence
it called forth.

But I understand the power
I *do* have;
I can tuck Franz's soul
away
inside a new dream.

I can give the artist
   another autumn day,
   another spring morning,
   another breath.
I can give them
  the life they dreamed
  one summer's night
  when only the stars
    (and I)
  were watching.

First, though,
I have to ask permission.

I'd never do to Franz
what Richter did to *me*.

**What I whisper**
against Franz's bruised lips:

*Do you want to live,*
  *even if it's not as a human being?*

*Do you want to live,*

*even if you'd be guiding souls*

*at my side?*

*Do you want to live,*

*even though your new life*

*will be strange?*

Franz sighs . . .
and says one final word.

*Yes.*

**I reach**
into Franz
and into myself.

All manner of things

s p i l l

from the artist's dying mind.
A pallet covered in rainbows of hope,
the notes of their sister's last song,
lost pages of equally lost books,
the sunshine in a place
called Jerusalem.

But a dream shared

between friends,

between lovers

is not easily lost.
I grasp

the feel of the wind
running its fingers
along a fox's spine,
the sound of the forest floor
giving beneath its paws.

I grasp
the years, the decades
Franz dreamed
of living.
It is not Odin's eternity
       (and maybe
         not even mine)
but it is a life
nonetheless.

I drape these dreams
around Franz.
And like a bird
sailing from a dovecote,
the artist emerges—
       shining
         and new.

**I take nothing for myself**
from this interlude of my life.

Let the silk shoes and dresses
fall to dust;

let the memory of me
grow dim
in Richter's ever-dying castle.

I leave here
with only one thing:
a pair of swan wings.
I place them beneath the painting
of Franz and I
at Neuschwanstein.

Ludwig may never claim them.
He may tuck them away
in a wardrobe, a chest,
his own broken heart;
he may stay a (human) king.

Or he may take back his magic
and find a love
who embraces all that he is.

I hope
he chooses
the same path
I have.

## Chapter Seventy-Three

**My heart is a compass,**
my true north
the woods
and presence of someone
like me: Franz.

Wrapped in flame-colored fur,
Franz looks more like themself
than they did
when they were (fully) human.
They will be with me until
we walk, leap, fly
to the Other Wood
at the end of our (shared) days,
our singular forever.

Franz and I are
a streak of starlight
breaking through the night,
a flash of sunrise
on the horizon.
We are a swan and a fox,
our own Wild Hunt, reborn.

*What if we meet*
*another hunter*
*like Richter?* Franz asks.

The wind sings
and so do I.
*We will defeat them.*
*We're fast; we're clever.*
*We can call on magic*
*whenever we choose.*
*We can shift and change*
*however we like.*
>          (Am I speaking
>          in a human tongue
>          or in the language of beasts?
>          I'm so much of both.
>          But I accept that now
>          and all the gifts
>          my duality brings me.)

*We won't be caged again.*
*And we will*
>          *always*
>                    *have*
>                              *each other.*

**We enter the forest**
and the dawn
together.

**The End**

# Acknowledgments

A thousand thanks to Ashley Hearn for her masterful editing skills and dedication to helping Hilde's story soar, and to the incredible publicity team at Peachtree Publishing and Holiday House, past and present: Darby Guinn, Sara DiSalvo, and Aleah Gornbein.

This book wouldn't exist without my agent Rena Rossner's friendship, unflagging patience, and guidance. And it would never would have been finished without Jacob, who walked out of Hell with me to look upon the stars, and made some terrible puns along the way. *Mir veln zey iberlebn.*

My gratitude goes to Dr. Steven D. Reece, whose kindness allowed me to find the courage to change my life and speak the truth in these pages, and to Andrzej and Natalia Stanisławska, for reminding me that the world is more than just a dark wood with their generosity.

*A Warning About Swans* was written during a stormy period of my life, and Celyta Jackson and feline residents of the Cat Cafe South Beach provided me with a lighthouse I could always return to. I'm forever grateful.

King Henry VIII, where would I be without your licks and your bites and your refusal to move off my lap when I'm supposed to be working? You are the best of cats and companions.

River, you are the Persephone to my Tisiphone. *Nolite te Bastardes Carborundorum.*

Celeste Gleason, thank you for trusting me with your journey and helping me with mine. Your guidance has shaped me into a better writer and person. I'm not just the woman with the sword anymore; I can carry a lantern now too.

To my family, I appreciate you reading multiple, *multiple* drafts of this book (one day, I promise not to make so many typos!) and bearing with me as I spent most of your vacation hunched over a keyboard.

Thank you to Roselle Lim, who celebrated every success with me and consoled me through every disappointment, and Li Wren, who fills my Friday nights with laughter, understanding, and cat antics.

Kip Wilson, Josh Gauthier, and Sarah Porter, the thoughtful feedback all of you gave me on early drafts of this novel helped make it infinitely better. Your insights were invaluable!

And finally, I'm humbled to have such a fairy-tale wonder of a cover thanks to Daria Hlazatova. *Slava Ukraini!*

## About the Author

**R. M. Romero** is a Jewish Latina and author of fairy tales for children and adults. She lives in Miami Beach with her cat, Henry VIII, and spends her summers helping to maintain Jewish cemeteries in Poland. You can visit her online at *RMRomero.com*.